Cousin Carrie

Keep a Good Heart

A Story for the Merry Christmas Time

Cousin Carrie

Keep a Good Heart
A Story for the Merry Christmas Time

ISBN/EAN: 9783744727655

Printed in Europe, USA, Canada, Australia, Japan

Cover: Foto ©Andreas Hilbeck / pixelio.de

More available books at **www.hansebooks.com**

THE ERRAND BOY BRINGING "FAITH."

"KEEP A GOOD HEART."

A Story

FOR

THE MERRY CHRISTMAS TIME.

·

BY

COUSIN CARRIE.

NEW YORK:
D. APPLETON AND COMPANY,
443 & 445 BROADWAY.
LONDON: 16 LITTLE BRITAIN.
1864.

"KEEP A GOOD HEART."

CHAPTER I.

"I AM sorry for you, Lilian, but they say the change must be made, and, much as I regret, I am unable to prevent it."

The speaker, a tall, grave-looking, middle-aged man, was principal of the public school in a small New England village. The words were addressed to a young girl not more than fifteen years of age, in deep mourning, who, with her head bowed upon the desk before which she was seated, and her whole frame quivering with suppressed sobs, seemed the very picture of helpless distress. The stern man's features lost much of their sternness, and something very like a tear shone for a moment in his usually cold gray eye, as he glanced from the weeping girl to a little child who stood by her side, crying because

her sister did, though she scarcely knew the
reason why. He moved uneasily, and hastily
repeated, " I am very sorry, Lilian."

The young girl arose, and, extending her
hand to him, said, with trembling lips,
" Thank you for your kind sympathy, Mr.
Wise. I know it is not in your power to
help me, or you would do so." Then hastily
tying on her bonnet, she took her little sister's hand, and, leaving the schoolhouse,
walked with a hurried step to a pretty little
cottage situated on the same street.

Lilian Ross was an orphan. Her father
died when she was but nine years old, her
brother Herbert fourteen, and little Eva a
beautiful blue-eyed baby. In less than a year
after his father's death, Herbert went away
on a sea voyage with an uncle. The ship
was lost on its homeward trip, and all on board
perished.

Mrs. Ross with her remaining children
continued to reside in the little white cottage
which had long been their home, until about
six months previous to the time at which our
story commences, when, after a long sickness,
she died, leaving her young daughters alone
in the world, penniless and almost friendless.

Lilian soon learned that, as the annuity
upon which they had hitherto lived ceased at

her mother's death, she must do something for the support of herself and little Eva, and hearing that an assistant teacher in the village school was about leaving, she applied for the situation, which, notwithstanding her youth, was readily granted her, for she had been a favorite pupil in the school, and all felt sympathy for her in her unprotected situation.

The cottage was taken by a nice, motherly old lady, Mrs. Smith, and her daughter. They had been friends of Mrs. Ross, and were much attached to her children. Lilian and Eva boarded with them, so they were not obliged to leave their old home; and though they sadly missed their mother, these kind friends did all in their power to supply her place; and if Lilian *did* sometimes feel very weary when the day's task was over, still she was happy in the thought that by her own exertion she was enabled to support herself and little sister in comfort.

But this Friday evening, Mr. Wise had asked her to remain a few moments after school, and when the children had all gone away with their merry voices and careless hearts, he told her that the school committee had decided that it would be necessary to have an older and more experienced teacher in her place, and that consequently, after the next week, which closed the fall term, her services would be no longer required.

The good man felt very sad at the pain he was obliged to inflict, and it is with his words of pity that our story opens.

With a sad heart Lilian performed the duties of her last week in school. Many a time did her tears blister the page of the primer from which some little child was laboriously lisping A, B, C, to the sorrowful surprise of the little one, who missed the encouraging smile of its young teacher.

Friday evening again came around. She received her quarter's salary from Mr. Wise, and for the last time crossed the threshold of the old red schoolhouse, where she had spent so many hours of happy childhood, and where she had had her first struggle with the cares and responsibilities of life.

The next day, Lilian sat by the windows of her own room, thinking sadly of the hard lot which had deprived her of her only support, and striving in vain to form some plan for the future. All was dark to her, and as the chilling ·November blast swept the few dead leaves from the 'naked branches, and the great drops of rain slowly trickled over the window pane, Nature seemed to have no message for her but of death, desolation, and tears.

Presently the door was thrown open and little Eva bounded into the room. She had quite forgotten the sorrow which she could not comprehend, and her bright eyes sparkled with pleasure, as she ran to her sister's side, holding up a few autumn flowers which she had found in a sheltered nook of their little garden.

Lilian tried to force an answering smile, but the child saw that she was too sad to share her delight in her treasures, and with a subdued look and quiet step, she stole away, and throwing herself on the rug before the fire, she commenced arranging her flowers. A very pretty picture was little Eva Ross as she sat there. Her bright curls, which lay in wild confusion over her black dress, shone in the firelight like burnished gold ; her cheeks were flushed with exercise, and her red lips parted with a smile of satisfaction as the bouquet grew beneath her skilful little fingers.

Presently she began to sing—at first in a low murmuring tone that did not arouse her sister from her sad musings; but soon her voice rose more clearly, and the words she sang became distinct.

Lilian turned to listen. A bright contrast was the happy child and her gay flowers to the dark clouds and bare tempest-tossed boughs upon which the young girl had been looking. And in as great contrast to her own foreboding thoughts was the simple song which the little one was singing.

> God bless the flowers, the gentle flowers,
>   That come to cheer us here ;
> They brighten many dusky hours,
>   And chide full many a tear.
>
> For will not He who keeps the flowers
>   Amid these autumn blasts, ·
> Protect us too, in darkening hours,
>   Until the storms are past ?

These trusting words, which little Eva sung in her artless way, stole like dawning light over the heart of her sister, awakening her sleeping faith and painting with the rainbow hues of hope the heavy clouds which hung around her spirit. She started up and catching the little warbler in her arms, covered her with kisses. Then she bathed her swollen eyes, resolving to waste no more time in useless tears, but to arouse herself and look about for some employment, however humble, that would bring them the necessities of life. Believing that He who had thus far provided for them would still continue his watchful care.

Eva was delighted to see her sister smile once more, and was soon prattling to her of the time she had gathering her flowers; how the wind almost blew her away and the rain splashed in her face. Then together they arranged the bright blossoms in their little blue vases, and were just admiring their handiwork, when Mrs. Smith came to tell Lilian that Miss Jackson wished to see her.

Miss Jackson was a cheerful, busy little body—the one dressmaker of B——, who knew every one in the village, a great many people out of it, and was a particular friend of good Mrs. Smith. When she heard that Lilian had lost her situation in the school, she was very indignant, and said more hard things of the trustees than her genial heart had ever thought or her smiling lips uttered before of any one. But her sympathy did not exhaust itself in words, as human sympathy is too apt to do: she determined, as she said, to "keep one eye open, and see if something would not turn up for the poor girl." Many a talk she and Mrs. Smith had on the subject. The latter would glady have kept the orphans with her free of charge, but she was poor herself, and could not gratify all her generous impulses.

And now Miss Jackson had come to announce that something *had* "turned up," in the shape of a New York milliner, who was
1*

visiting her brother, Deacon Sharp, and who
wished to find a young girl to go back to the
city with her and make herself generally useful in her establishment. Miss Jackson had
been at the Deacon's house fitting a dress for
Mrs. Sharp, and as the subject was discussed
in her hearing, she at once thought of Lilian,
and was so enthusiastic in her praise as to
convince Mrs. Pettigue that she would have
found an inestimable treasure, if the young
girl could be persuaded to accompany her.

It was accordingly agreed that the bustling little dressmaker should call on Lilian
that very day, and, if she was willing to try
city life, bring her to see her would-be employer.

Poor Lilian was much distressed at the
thought of leaving her quiet country home
and the dear friends who had shared her joys
and sympathized with her sorrows ; but she
must in some way support herself and Eva,
and it might be many a long day before she
could find employment in the village ; so driving back her tears, she prepared to accompany
Miss Jackson to the Deacon's.

Mrs. Smith wept bitterly as she thought
how lonely the cottage would be without little Eva's merry songs and laughter, and how
long the winter evenings would seem with no

Lilian to read aloud, while she and her daughter were busied with their sewing and knitting; and deeper than any selfish sorrow was the pain of seeing her darlings go forth from the safe shelter of her humble roof to wrestle with the trials and temptations of the great city. But she could not bid them stay; she could only pray that the Father of the fatherless would guide and guard them amid the dangers which would surround them when she should be no longer near to counsel and direct.

CHAPTER II.

THE interview between Mrs. Pettigue and
Lilian was very satisfactory to the former,
who congratulated herself upon her good fortune in having secured the services of so mod-
est and ladylike a girl; whose quiet, gentle
manners she felt sure would add another
charm to her already famous establishment.
But very far from satisfactory was the impression made upon poor Lilian by her new
acquaintance. Mrs. Pettigue was a thin, sallow woman, with restless, piercing black eyes,
that seemed ever on the alert to discover some
fault or failing in others. She was dressed in
the extreme of fashion, but no outward adorn-
ing could conceal her native vulgarity. When
conversing with the young orphan she inva-
riably spoke in the gentlest of tones, but with
so evident an effort, that Lilian readily guessed
it was not her usual manner of speaking to
those who were dependent upon her. Nor
was she far from right. There was enough

tyranny swelling in the heart which throbbed beneath Mrs. Pettigue's fashionably cut bodice, to have furnished the Czar of all the Russias, and the Emperor of Morocco to boot; and though her domain was small, her subjects were made to feel the weight of her iron scep're none the less keenly. But she was quick to perceive that Lilian possessed characteristics which, though not congenial to her own nature, were calculated to please many of the most influential of her patrons; and thinking that the fact of her having so pleasing an attendant in her rooms might result in an increase of custom, she was very anxious to secure her services, and so much overacted her *rôle* of disinterested benefactress that Lilian soon saw through the disguise. Still, as there seemed no alternative, she accepted her propositions, and after agreeing to return with her to New York the next week, left the good Deacon's house, with a heavier heart even than that with which she had entered. Not so with gay, hopeful, little Miss Jackson : she was too single-minded herself to suspect another of duplicity, and too blind with regard to the faults of her neighbors, to discover aught else in the honest Deacon's sister than that she was a very obliging body, who had given her some valuable

information about the fashions, and finally
had quite won her heart by speaking so kindly to Lilian, and providing her with so good
a situation; and though she could not help
feeling sad at the thought of so soon parting
with her and her little pet Eva, she reproved
herself for what she called her selfishness, and
as they walked homeward, in the cold drizzling rain, she talked cheeringly and hopefully
to her young companion, of the future, which
she was determined should be bright, and how,
one of these days, when she had made her fortune in New York, she and little Eva would
come back to dear old B——, and they should
all be so happy as to quite forget that they
had ever been sorrowful.

Lilian listened and tried to feel encouraged
and to answer in the same cheerful strain, but
a choking sensation in her throat would not
let her speak, so she walked on in silence, and
in silence she returned the good-night kiss of
her cheery, bustling friend, at the gate of the
little cottage.

Little Eva was the only one of the household whose sleep was undisturbed that night.
Mrs. Smith and her daughter lay awake, vainly trying to form some plan by which the
parting might be avoided, and when at last
they were forced to relinquish this hope, their

thoughts were kept busy with self-denying plans to furnish the young orphans with a comfortable outfit for their journey.

"There is my bombazine dress, Rebecca," said the old lady; "it was bought when your father died, and that is ten long years ago. The waist and sleeves are pretty much gone, and I was thinking of having the skirt made into a petticoat this winter; but perhaps it is most too good for that, and there is enough of it to make Eva a dress and sacque. When it is sponged and pressed it will look very nice. I will see Miss Jackson about it to-morrow. If she will cut and fit the dress, we can manage the rest ourselves."

To this Miss Becky readily agreed; then after a moment's reflection, she said, "And mother, you know I am having my black delaine, made over; Miss Jackson fitted the new lining yesterday, but really I go out so little I hardly need it. With a little altering she can make it a very nice dress for Lilian."

Mrs. Smith thought over her daughter's already scanty wardrobe, and demurred at her making the sacrifice; but her objection was soon overruled by Miss Becky, who declared that she could do so well without the dress that she wondered she had ever thought of having it made up for herself.

Thus, with noble self-forgetfulness, the mother and daughter through many hours of the night were wakeful and busy with economical but generous contrivances for the comfort of their dear ones, and even when at last they fell asleep, dreamed of footing stockings and knitting mittens for them.

Think you not that the recording angel who bent above the couch of those two poor women, noting down their little self-sacrifices, bore to the courts of heaven as bright a page as that which chronicled the millionaire's gift of thousands to some popular charity?

While her kind friends were thus striving to forget their own grief in planning for her welfare, Lilian, relieved from the restraint, which, for their sake and that of little Eva, she had placed upon herself when with the family, wept and sobbed most bitterly. Forgetting that she had resolved so short a time before never more to despond, but always to put her trust in God, she now looked despairingly upon the darkest spot in her unpromising future, and felt that she was utterly forsaken. The loud striking of the old clock as it marked the slowly passing hours, seemed now a knell for the happy days that were gone, and now an alarm, warning her of those which were approaching. It was not until the gray morning light looked in at her chamber window that the wearied and excited girl found sweet forgetfulness in sleep.

The few remaining days of the orphans' stay in their old home were so fully occupied with the hurried preparations for their departure, that there was but little time to give way to unavailing regrets. A few friends came to bid them good-by, and express their good wishes for their future. Together they visited a few favorite spots, and knelt at their parents' graves, but all was done hurriedly and in a kind of excitement which prevented the full realization that it was the last time, it might be for years, and it might be forever, that they were to look upon these dear scenes and faces which had so long been familiar to them.

CHAPTER III.

TIME moves with no laggard pace when he bears us onward to some dreaded future, however distant it may seem, and Lilian's little week of respite flew past on such rapid wings that before she had learned fully to comprehend the fact that she was to go forth in the wide cold world, the appointed day had arrived. The last stitch had been taken in the humble outfit; the trunk—she and Eva needed but one—stood ready locked and strapped ; her bonnet and shawl lay on the snowy counterpane of the bed where she had dreamed childhood's bright dreams, and beside which she had knelt to ask for strength to bear the sorrows that pressed so heavily on her youth. Mrs. Smith with trembling hands was stowing away in a little basket the nice things which were to beguile their journey, and Miss Becky was for the last time smoothing little Eva's curls, while her tears, which fell like rain upon the golden ripples, so blinded her that she could hardly see to perform the loving task. Nothing remained but to look once more into the room where her mother died, and say the last sad words of farewell to those who had so faithfully endeavored to fill her place. Bravely she strove against the feeling of utter desolation that chilled her very heart; but when old Ponto, who had been the playmate of her childhood, came and thrust his shaggy head in her lap, and gazing into her face with a wistful, inquiring look, as if he suspected she was about to leave him, and would reproach her for the desertion, her forced fortitude gave way, and throwing her arms around the neck of the old favorite, she wept bitterly.

Little Eva, who had been secretly instructed by Miss Jackson to "be a good girl, and not give her sister any trouble, and on no account to let her see that she was sorry to leave the old place, but to keep singing and playing about as if nothing was the matter," had all the morning been striving to carry out the somewhat difficult part assigned her, thereby gaining for herself the reputation with some of the neighbors of being a "heartless little minx, who cared no more about leaving her old friends than if they were so many stocks and stones." Little did those who judged her know that the child loved even the very "stocks and stones" about the humble homestead with an ardor which they were incapable of appreciating, and that the songs which gave such offence came welling wearily up from a heart which longed to give vent to its grief in childish lamentations ; that what they condemned as heartlessness, was smiled upon by good angels as an evidence of noble self-forgetfulness. But Eva's self-control, heroically as she had struggled for it, deserted her at last ; for when she saw her sister weeping on the neck of old Ponto, the grief which she had so long kept tightly locked in her baby heart, burst forth in passionate sobs. Miss Becky caught the child to her breast and mingled her tears with those of her little favorite, and kind-hearted Mrs. Smith strove with trembling lips to speak the words of comfort which she could not feel.

"Hoity, toity ! what is all this about ?" exclaimed Deacon Sharp, who had come up with his light wagon to convey the young travellers together with his sister to the nearest railroad station, and who, entering without knocking, had come upon the little household at the moment they were thus giving vent to their grief at parting. "Why, Lillie," he continued, "one would think that Pont was your last friend, and about to suffer a just

penalty on the gallows for all the robberies of
my henroost that he has been guilty of.
Cheer up, child! I promise you, I will not
touch a hair of his wicked old head while you
are gone. And you too, rosebud!" (toss-
ing Eva in the air,) "take care, you will put
out those bright eyes, and then you can't see
the fine sights when you get to York."

The blunt but good-natured Deacon did
much toward restoring the composure of the
sorrowful group, for there is no surer check
to the outward manifestation of grief than
that which it receives from the unsympa-
thizing though not unfriendly ridicule or jest.

The brief farewells were hurried through,
and Lilian soon found herself seated beside
Mrs. Pettigue, who looked with ill-concealed
impatience upon her pale face and swollen
eyes, and who, instead of speaking words of
comfort and encouragement, began almost immediately to tell her how foolish she was, not
to follow her advice and leave Eva behind,
dwelling on the burden and hinderance she
would be to her in the city, and assuring her
that she would never consent to have the
child loitering about her rooms. Poor Lilian
listened to the fretful tirade in silence, seeing
in it but the beginning of trouble, and half
condemning herself for taking her little sis-

ter to share the dreary lot which she saw
opening before her.

When they reached the cars, all was
noise and confusion, and the youthful travellers, bewildered by the novel sight and sounds,
scarcely heard the Deacon's hearty good-by,
or realized that they were flying with almost
the swiftness of thought away from their happy home.

Mrs. Pettigue, to whom a ride on the railroad was no new thing, ensconced herself
comfortably in a corner of the seat, and gave
her attention wholly to the perusal of the last
new novel. Little Eva, relieved from the sur-
veillance of those piercing black eyes, knelt
by the window, and with childhood's elasticity of spirit, forgot her grief in wondering
admiration of the varied scenes which flitted
before her gaze. Thus left to herself, Lilian
drew her veil closely over her face and lost
all consciousness of outward things in moody,
troubled thought.

The incongruous party were borne swiftly
on their journey, and reached New York early
in the evening—a dark, chill, drizzling evening—the atmosphere redolent of a gassy odor,
the pavements slippery with a muddy slime,
the men, women, and children who thronged
the streets wearing on their brows a discon-

tented, gloomy frown, or a careworn look that told of a life of anxiety and toil. Forlorn indeed was the first impression of the city received by the orphans, who had never before been ten miles from their quiet village home.

They mechanically followed Mrs. Pettigue into the omnibus which was to take them within a short distance of her boarding house, where they were to remain for the night, and until other accommodations could be found for them. Poor little Eva clung to her sister in terror as the noisy, unwieldy vehicle dashed recklessly through the crowded streets, while Lilian feeling all the utter hopelessness of first homesickness, almost wished that some catastrophe might put an end to that life which she imagined had forever lost all charms for her.

The next morning all things seemed to wear a more hopeful aspect. Lilian, having wept herself to sleep the night before, began to feel something of the reaction which usually follows any violent demonstration of emotion, whether it be of joy or grief, and looked with growing interest upon the strange city sights to which her excited little sister, who had taken her stand at the window, was continually calling her attention. The sun shone brightly through the ragged openings of the

fast retreating clouds, casting its cheerful
light over the scene which had seemed so
gloomy the previous evening.

It had been decided before they left B——
that, if they could procure rooms, it would be
better for them to take lodgings in some
quiet, respectable neighborhood, as they
could in that way live more economically,
and (which was a great consideration with
good Mrs. Smith) in greater seclusion than at
some third or fourth-rate boarding house,
which would be the best that their means
could provide. Accordingly, on this, the
first morning after their arrival, Mrs. Pettigue told Lilian that she should not expect
her to enter upon the duties of her new calling until the following day, but would send
to her one of the girls in her employ, whose
mother sometimes had furnished rooms to let,
as she thought there could be some arrangement made for their accommodation there.

Ellen Havens, for whose visit Lilian was
thus prepared, was a lively, thoughtless girl,
naturally kind hearted, but as she was governed entirely by impulse, her quickly formed
friendships were not of a very abiding character. She was charmed by the beauty of
her new acquaintance, and touched by her
air of sadness. Little Eva she pronounced a

most bewitching little fairy, and almost devoured the astonished child with kisses, while
she enumerated the advantages of her mother's rooms, and expatiated on the happiness
in store for them all when they should form
one household, though she added, with a
shrug of the shoulders, that Mrs. Pettigue's
evil temper was a sad drawback to the fe-
licity of any unfortunate mortal who was
placed in her power.

Lilian listened almost in silence, as they
walked toward Mrs. Havens's, to Ellen's
graphic description of the " scenes" which
were sometimes enacted in Mrs. Pettigue's
work rooms. Her heart failed her as she
heard this evidence in confirmation of her
own preconceived opinion of her employer,
which, under the influence of the cheerful
sunlight, she had begun to hope was unjust.

The mother of Ellen was a fretful, careworn looking woman, a decided contrast to
her sprightly daughter. She had seen better
days, and never ceased to lament her changed
fortunes. Her clouded brow and complaining voice raised a perpetual protest against
the hard fate which had banished her from a
life of ease and comfort to one of toil and
privation; but though she mourned for the
past, she did not fail to do what she could to

2

supply the necessities of the present. When, by her husband's death, she was left with three little children to provide for, and found that, after the estate was settled, the only property remaining to her was the house and furniture, she decided to take boarders, as the sole means open to her by which she could support the family.

For a time she succeeded very well, but in a few years the neighborhood was so changed by the encroachments of business, that she found it difficult to procure a sufficient number of boarders of a class that she was willing to receive. Accordingly she was induced to rent some of her rooms to one or two respectable families, whose means would not allow them either to board or to occupy a whole house by themselves.

Poor Mrs. Havens had many trials, but the bitterest of all was that, in spite of her exertions, she could not save her children from rough contact with the world. It was a sad day to her when she gave her reluctant consent that Ellen, her eldest daughter, should accept an offered situation at Mrs. Pettigue's; but long and expensive illness had not only exhausted her slender purse, but added debt to their other perplexities. It was necessary something should be done, and Ellen, with her usual impulsiveness, was eager to try her hand at making the beautiful things which so charmed her in the milliner's windows.

She had been in the employ of Mrs. Pettigue for nearly a year when Lilian made her acquaintance, and had long since discovered that the lot she had chosen was a hard one. Many a time did she look with envy upon the fair purchaser of some "love of a bonnet" which she herself had helped to form. Ah! she knew not that the costliest lace and flowers might shade a brow throbbing with an anguish deeper than any she had yet fathomed, or perhaps she would have murmured less.

It was soon arranged that Lilian and little Eva should become the occupants of Mrs. Havens's vacant apartments—a third-story back room of moderate size, with a smaller one opening from it, which would do very well for a bedroom; the larger one was to serve as parlor and dining room all in one. A kitchen Lilian said they could very well dispense with, for she must be "maid of all work," and would certainly have no time to cook.

Both rooms were furnished neatly, though plainly, and when the windows were draped

with the pretty chintz curtains which Mrs.
Smith had insisted Lilian should take, because
they had been her mother's, they had quite a
cosy appearance.

In the course of the afternoon, Mrs. Havens, who felt quite an interest in the young
orphans, offered to go out with them if there
were any purchases they wished to make.
Lilian gladly accepted the offer. The remains
of the lunch which Mrs. Smith had prepared
for them the day before served very well in
place of dinner, but it was necessary she
should buy something for supper, and she
was almost afraid to venture into the
crowded streets alone.

Their first visit was to a china store,
which, though a very unpretending establishment for the city, filled our little country-bred
Eva with admiration. While her sister, with
the advice and assistance of Mrs. Havens, was
selecting the few cups and plates which were
absolutely necessary for their use, she strayed
off by herself, gazing in unutterable delight
upon the beautiful objects which surrounded
her. She fancied that she was in Fairyland,
and that the bright flakes of prismatic light,
which fell upon her from a large cut-glass
vase in the window, were real, tangible jewels
with which the fairies were decking her. She

stooped to let the bright shower fall on her golden curls, and bared one white, plump arm to see how the quivering gems would become it. But suddenly she forgot her fantastic play, for her roving eye chanced to rest on a little Parian figure, more beautiful than anything even her beauty-loving little heart had ever dreamed of. It represented a child standing on the sea beach. On one side loomed up a barren rock, on the other the foam-crested waves dashed even to her feet, while her garments and hair were wildly tossed by the tempest. Her dimpled hands pressed a cross tightly to her breast, and the upturned face wore an expression of sweet, calm trust, in striking and beautiful contrast to the marks of violence and desolation which the other portions of the work evinced. On the brow rested one of the rainbow-hued rays with which little Eva had been toying.

The child gazed in silent rapture, while her bosom heaved and her eyes filled with tears whose source she could not have told. Presently she drew nearer, and, mounting a high stool that stood by the shelf on which rested this creation of an art which seems almost divine, she pressed her full, warm lips on the still, calm brow of the image, murmuring to herself low and lovingly, "Beautiful, beautiful!"

"Here, little girl ! hands off ! " exclaimed a rough voice. At the same time she was lifted, not very gently, from her seat and placed upon the floor. Terrified and abashed, she cast one timid glance at the frowning face of her reprover, and then looked wildly around for Lilian. Just then a hand was laid protectingly on her head, and, raising her tearful eyes, she perceived a gentleman with a kind, benevolent face bending over her, and saying to the angry shopman :

"Let the little one look, if it gives her pleasure. I will see that she injures nothing."

The nervous proprietor of fragile merchandise bowed deferentially, and, hastening away to attend a customer, left the field to Eva and her champion.

The gentleman placed her again on the seat from which she had been so unceremoniously deposed, and with kind and gentle words soon succeeded in dispelling the cloud which had momentarily cast its shadow over her bright brow.

"So you admire this little marble girl, do you, Eva ? " asked her new friend, placing his hand on the figure, upon which her eyes had been fixed while she answered the questions he had put regarding her name and home.

She raised her eyes to his face, and replied.

earnestly, "I love it, oh! so dearly! I never saw anything so beautiful before. I shall never, never forget it;" and again the little enthusiast bent down and kissed the "thing of beauty," the very remembrance of which would be to her "a joy forever." ·

The gentleman smiled with an expression half amused, half sad; then, taking the child's little hand in his, he continued, "Has she no message for you, Eva?"

She looked up at first with a puzzled air, then her lips half parted, but she made no reply.

"Tell me, my child, do you know what this figure represents?" he repeated.

"Yes, sir," said Eva. "It is a little girl on the sea shore. The great high rock will not let her go that way, and here the sea is sending its waves dashing against her. The bright sky is all covered up with wild, black clouds; the lightning flashes as if the heavens were on fire, and the thunder, the sea, and the wind fill the whole air with dreadful noise—"

"Wait, my child," interrupted the gentleman with a smile, "How do you know all this? Here we have the little girl, and the rock, and the waves, to be sure, but why do you think that there are clouds hanging above, and storms raging around her?" ·

" I can tell there is a storm, because, see how her hair and her dress are tossed by the wind; and I know how dreadful it is, for I was on the beach in a thunder storm once with mamma. Oh, it was awful; I was so frightened that I screamed and cried. But this little girl is better than I—she remembers who made the sea and the rocks, who guides the clouds and the lightning—she hears sweet music in the sound of the thunder and the roaring of the waves, for God is speaking to her."

The little hands which had been moving in nervous gestures, dropped passively in her lap, and the flushed face, quivering with excitement, was reverently bowed as the child ceased speaking. Her companion looked at her in amazement. Was this the same child that he had watched but a moment ago playing with a sunbeam, now translating so eloquently the beautiful hieroglyph which he had thought far beyond her comprehension? He laid his hand on her head, and smoothing back her curls, said in a low, grave voice :

" Little Eva, listen to the lesson which this image of Faith should teach you. When distress surrounds you, and dangers threaten, you must not, as you did at the sea beach, give way to helpless terror, but, like her, look upward and see a Father's hand beckoning through the tempest. The path of life lies through many a rocky pass, but do not fear; though the chilling waves of sorrow and trouble dash over you, have faith in God; know that He doeth all things well."

He had spoken as if forgetful how young a child was his auditor, and to many of her age his words might have been unintelligible; but there was a thoughtful little brain under those golden ringlets, and not only did she understand the words of the stranger, but her young heart thrilled with the new thoughts and resolves which they awakened. She had been taught to believe that God was ever near, watching all her actions and guiding all her ways, but never before had she so realized it, and she rejoiced in the thought that she could hear and follow her Heavenly Father's call, even though it must be through the tempest.

She looked up, and replied slowly and earnestly, "I don't think I shall ever be afraid of anything in the wide world again."

The gentleman smiled somewhat sadly; she saw it, and her lips parted as if to speak, but just then her sister called her. Turning to "little Faith," she bestowed a caress in which was mingled fondness and a feeling

2*

akin to reverence. Then demurely giving her
hand to her new friend, she slid from the ele-
vated seat, and the next moment was with
Lilian and Mrs. Havens, once more in the
street. The new sights and sounds by which
she was surrounded, drove the incident in the
china store from her thoughts for the time
being, and she enjoyed vastly the dignity and
responsibility of carrying the basket, in which
were deposited, as they were purchased, the
simple viands that were to constitute their
supper, and breakfast for the next morning.

When they reached home, she was so
tired with the long walk and excitement, that
she was quite content to sit on a low seat by
the fire with her doll in her arms, and watch
her sister as she placed the little tea kettle on
the stove, and spread on the table the snowy
damask, which, as well as the curtains, had
been their mother's. But when Lilian un-
rolled the spoons marked with that mother's
name, and placed them on the table, her eyes
filled with tears as she contrasted the happy
past, of which they were mementoes, with the
lonely, cheerless present. She turned away to
hide her grief from little Eva ; but the child's
quick ear caught the half-audible sigh, and
stealing to her side, she whispered, " Don't
feel bad—don't cry, Lilian."

LILIAN IN HER NEW HOME.

Yet when her eye fell upon the simple household treasures of the old homestead, the chilling feeling of loneliness and homesickness crept over her heart too. For one moment she struggled with the fast-rising tears, and then, kneeling by her sister's side, she sobbed as if her heart would break.

Lilian raised her to her lap, and locked in each other's arms, the orphans wept. Lilian was the first to recover herself; hastily brushing away her tears, she exclaimed :

" There, darling! I have spoiled all your pleasant day with my selfish tears. Come, birdie, dry your eyes, and we will try to talk of something cheerful."

The child was soon comforted, but in a moment she turned to her sister and asked :

" It isn't wicked to cry, is it, Lilian ? "

" Why, no, little sister. Why do you ask such a question ? "

" Because I thought once to-day that it would be, and that I should never cry again; but being sorry isn't like being afraid to trust God, is it ? "

Lilian shook her head—she could not trust her voice to reply.

" No, it can't be wrong, Lillie," continued the child, " for if we were never sorry for anything, how could we tell whether we

trusted Him or not? If we hadn't any
trouble we couldn't be like little Faith, could
we?"

"Who is little Faith, Eva?" asked Lilian,
somewhat puzzled. And the little girl was
soon giving an animated description of the
beautiful figure, and the kind gentleman she
had seen at the china store. While she was
yet talking, there came a rap at the door.
Eva sprang to open it, admitting a boy with
a huge basket containing the dishes which
Lilian had purchased, and for which they
were waiting supper.

Eva was delighted, and her sister looked
on with some satisfaction as the boy placed
one article after another carefully on the carpet. At last he handed out a pretty painted
mug, and the number was complete. Eva
thought it very beautiful, and when she saw
the words " For my little sister," written in
gilt letters within the delicate rose wreath,
she knew it was for her, and bounding to her
sister's side, she almost smothered her with
kisses.

The errand boy stood looking on with a
good-natured grin, then, again turning to his
basket, he produced something carefully
wrapped up; removing the wrappings he
placed on the table—what do you think?

Eva could hardly believe her eyes, but it was " beautiful little Faith."

" There is some mistake," Lilian said to the boy; " this does not belong here."

" I guess it does—leastwise, boss told me to leave it here 'long with them things," and with an awkward bow, he disappeared down the stairs.

Eva's delight and amazement kept her silent, till Lilian, bent upon solving the mystery, discovered a card attached to the figure, on which was written, " For little Eva, from one who has walked far in the stony path, and knows that Faith can make bright the darkest days."

" Why, birdie," she exclaimed, " this must be from your new friend."

" Is it really for me, sister, and did the kind gentleman send it to me ? "

" It is certainly for you, for here is your name, and I know of no one who could have sent it but the kind gentleman, as you call him."

The child sat for some moments gazing upon her treasure, too full of happiness for words, then throwing her arms around it, she exclaimed, " Oh! Lilian, arn't you glad that dear, beautiful Faith has come to live with us ? ".

Lilian answered her with a kiss, but it

was long ere the artless question left her thoughts. It would ever return linked with the words which the friendly stranger's hand had written on the card. Was it true that faith could brighten earthly sorrows? If she received the heavenly guest into her heart as gladly and lovingly as her little sister received the image, would *her* trials seem lighter?

The little room had a very cheerful look when the curtains were drawn, the gas lighted, and the table set with the pretty new dishes. Then Lilian cut the baker's loaf (which Eva declared was no larger than one of Aunty Smith's biscuits), and made some nice brown toast, while Eva, anxious to be useful, placed on the table the chipped beef and little cakes which had formed part of the contents of the basket which she had been so proud to carry; then the tea sent forth its fragrant aroma, as Lilian poured it into the graceful little tea-pot, and the orphans sat down to the first meal of their own preparing.

Eva was in high spirits—she could hardly drink her tea for looking at the roses on the mug, and she had so much to say about the kind stranger and his beautiful gift, that she almost forgot to eat her cake. Lilian could not but catch some of the spirit of gladness that glanced from her little sister's bright eyes. They had quite a merry time of it, washing the dishes and arranging them in the closet, and on the whole, the evening passed away much more pleasantly than she would have believed it possible that her first evening in the city could have done. At last, little Eva began to show unmistakable symptoms of having sat up beyond her usual bedtime. Her merry prattle was hushed, and the fringed curtains would fall over her blue eyes, in spite of all her efforts. When she was undressed, and stood in her long white night dress beside her sister, who was waiting to hear her repeat her evening prayer, she said, in a low sweet voice :

" Lillie, may I ask God to bless the good gentleman who sent sweet little Faith ? " and the orphaned child, kneeling for the first time in her new home, prayed for a blessing upon the stranger whose kindness had made her little heart so glad.

Eva had just fallen asleep, when Ellen Havens came to the room with a message from Mrs. Pettigue, that she should expect Lilian punctually at her place in the morning. She seemed quite delighted at the thought of having her for a companion in her early walk, and chatted and laughed so merrily, that she gave her no time to indulge the foreboding thoughts which the mention of Mrs. Pettigue's name aroused.

CHAPTER IV.

VERY early the next morning the orphans were astir. Their frugal breakfast was soon despatched, the rooms put in order, and they were ready to go on their separate ways to encounter the great untried world. For little Eva, as well as her sister, was to meet strange faces and learn new duties.

The younger children of Mrs. Havens attended a public school not far distant, and it was agreed that she should accompany them. Lilian's anxiety about her was greatly relieved by the arrangement, as she had felt much disturbed at the thought of leaving her alone at home, during the long hours of her daily absence; and though the child herself felt some heart quakings at the prospect before her, she carefully hid her fears from her sister, and talked merrily and hopefully of how much she would learn, and how very good she would be at school.

The breakfast things were just washed

and returned to the closet shelves, when Ellen's voice was heard at the door bidding Lilian "make haste, or they would be late, and catch a lecture from Mrs. Pettigue." Hurriedly throwing on her bonnet and shawl, she gave the child one kiss, and a last injunction to be a good girl, and then was gone.

Finding herself alone, Eva's fears returned with greater force, and bowing her head on the table, she burst into tears. Presently, chancing to look up, her eyes fell upon the little image of Faith: instantly she remembered all the resolutions of yesterday, and feeling rebuked, she dried her eyes and turned to the window, hoping to find some object of interest to divert her attention from her own troubles, and help her to keep down the rebellious sobs.

As the little child watched the gray clouds slowly dispersing before the rising sun, her mind was busy with thoughts of Him who made them, and though she was ignorant of the origin of the clouds, and thought that the sun was really moving, yet she left the window wiser than many a world-renowned philosopher, for Nature had repeated the lesson that the beautiful work of Art had whispered, and faith had taken deeper root in her young heart.

When John and Jennie Havens came to
call her at school time, they found her busy
dressing her doll—the terror was all gone;
and no one who saw her as she trudged by
Jennie's side, with her little dinner basket in
her hand, would have dreamed that those
bright eyes had been so lately dimmed with
tears.

Of her two companions she liked Jennie
best. She was three or four years her senior,
and quite inclined to act the part of patron
and champion toward the little stranger. To
be sure, she was somewhat selfish and dictato-
rial, and expected her *protegée* to be governed
entirely by her will; but then she would not
allow any one else to tyrannize over her, and
Eva was for the present willing to pay the
tribute of obedience to her whims, in order to
secure the protection of so powerful an ally;
for John, a stout boy of twelve or thirteen,
began already to show a decided inclination
to tease and annoy the helpless little girl,
which his sister's threats and expostulations
alone kept in check.

When they reached the school, she was
very glad to find that his place of destination
was in quite a different part of the building
from hers, and that the class to which she was
conducted was in the same room with Jen-

nic. And though she could not help con-
trasting the frowning brow, and harsh, sharp
voice of the teacher to whose care she was
consigned, with the mild looks and sweet
voice of her sister, who had until now been
her only instructor, still she felt that, after all,
going to a new school, though perhaps not
the pleasantest thing in the world, was not
quite so bad as she had imagined.

Now we will leave little Eva perched on
a high bench, industriously striving to fix her
wandering thoughts on the book before her,
and will follow Lilian to her new field of
duty. She and Ellen reached Mrs. Pettigue's
in time to escape the-dreaded lecture. Indeed, that lady was in less of a lecturing
mood this morning, than usual, and received
them quite graciously.

Ellen went to her place in the workroom,
while Mrs. Pettigue herself conducted Lilian
to the salesrooms, and explained what would
be required of her.

The poor girl was sadly confused by the
curious glances which the shopgirls cast
toward her, and her embarrassment was not
lessened as she overheard their whispered criti-
cisms of her dress and appearance. But as the
morning wore away, and the rooms became
filled with ladies, all eager to be first served,

she found so much to do that she had no time to
think of herself, and consequently her timidity
soon disappeared, and she even became interested in the busy scene. Mrs. Pettigue, though
seemingly forgetful of her, watched her narrow-
ly. It was well Lilian did not know that those
piercing black eyes were following her, or she
would hardly have won the golden opinions
which were silently showered upon her, both
by the milliner and her customers.

The busy day at last drew to a close, and
Lilian was surprised to find how quickly it
had passed, and how few trials it had brought
her. A brisk walk through the brilliantly
lighted streets, and she was once more at her
new home. Eva, who had been alone ever
since her return from school, was delighted to
see her. She had the table set, and the kettle boiling, and considered herself quite a
smart housekeeper. Lilian praised her industry, and while she prepared tea, they re-
counted to each other their separate histories
of the day's experience.

Several weeks passed by with their mingled
joys and sorrows. Lilian's homesickness began to wear away. She had become quite a
favorite with a number of Mrs. Pettigue's
customers, who thought none could serve
them so well as the young girl, whose pa-

tience was never wearied by their fastidious-
ness, and whose exquisite taste and skilful
fingers were always ready to suggest improve-
ments and make alterations wherever required, without regard to her own ease.

Mrs. Pettigue, pleased with her popularity, treated her with much more consideration than she did the other girls. But Lilian
found to her sorrow, as many a favorite had
found before, that the favor of those in authority brings with it annoyance and danger
as well as benefit. The indulgence which
spared her many a harsh word and unjust
reproof from the head of the establishment,
won for her the jealousy and dislike of those
who were to be her daily associates. Even
Ellen was less friendly than at first. Lilian
noticed the change, but for a time could not
guess the cause. One morning, however, she
accidentally overheard a conversation between
Ellen and one of the other girls, from which
she discovered that they looked upon her with
suspicion, on account of Mrs. Pettigue's partiality, even fancying that she was set as a
spy over them.

In vain she strove by every means in her
power to do away their unjust suspicions.
She could not but see that she was daily becoming more and more an object of aversion

to her companions. The loss of Ellen's friend-
ship was a sore trial. The wild, merry girl
had been the first one in the great city to
speak a cheering word to her, and had treated
her with kindness and attention. And Lilian,
wilfully blind to her many faults, had lavished
upon her much of that romantic affection
which young girls are so apt to bestow upon
those whom their own imagination has en-
dowed with most exalted virtues, but who are
really, perhaps, quite unworthy of their admiration.

Now that the delusion was over, she saw
her mistake, yet could not but mourn the
downfall of her bright ideal.

But much as she missed Ellen's society,
she had yet to learn that the loss of her fickle
friend was not the worst result of her unfortunate popularity.

Envy and jealousy are dangerous seeds to
sow in the human heart; in all, the fruit
must be evil; in some, perhaps only a rank
weed, which exhausts the good qualities of the
soil from which it springs; in others, a prickly
nettle, which stings and torments all who come
in contact with it; and in another, the poison-
ous nightshade, concealing under a fair exterior the most deadly venom.

So, with the evil passions which Mrs. Pettigue had aroused in the breasts of her employees by her unjust severity to them, coupled with the marked partiality wlfich she showed for Lilian, some envied what they considered her good fortune, and coveted her beauty and grace; others strove by petty annoyances to harass and provoke her; but there was one who, without any outward show of dislike, cherished a secret and bitter hatred for the young orphan.

Maria Roberts had been with Mrs. Pettigue three or four years, and for a long time stood high in that lady's good graces; but of late they had had many disagreements, and about the time of Lilian's arrival Mrs. Pettigue began very decidedly to withdraw her favor. Consequently, Maria had looked upon her from the first as a rival, and resolved to watch her opportunity for revenge. Opportunity to do wrong is seldom wanting long for those who seek it; and Maria's evil genius did not forsake her on this occasion, as we shall see.

One morning, when Lilian had been in the city little more than a month, Miss C——, one of Mrs. Pettigue's most valued customers, called to order a headdress, and to Maria fell the task of waiting on her. Now, Miss C—— was determined that for this particular even-

ing her coiffure should be decidedly unique,
and withal very becoming.

Maria exerted her skill to the utmost to
give satisfaction, but in vain ; the fastidious
beauty would not be pleased. This was too
commonplace, and that made her " look like
a fright." At last, turning impatiently to
Mrs. Pettigue, she exclaimed :

" Do send that young girl here who made
me that charming wreath last week. I am
sure she can contrive something. Lilian Ross
I think her name is."

Maria was instantly despatched to sum-
mon Lilian, her heart swelling with indignation, and more than ever thirsting for revenge
upon the innocent cause of her annoyance.

Lilian obeyed, with a sigh, the ungra-
ciously delivered command. She knew from
experience the exacting and capricious temper of the lady who was pleased to favor her
with her preference, and she also saw that she
herself was in some way the object of the
anger which was flashing in the dark eyes of
her companion ; but there was no time for questions or explanations, even if she could venture to attempt them. She was soon busied
with ribbons and lace, striving, in her turn, to
please the capricious belle. In this she was
more fortunate than Maria had been, and in a

short time had completed a headdress, which
even Miss C—— pronounced perfect; so
light, so airy and graceful—really there was
no fault to be found with it.

Lilian was in the act of adjusting the exquisite little affair on the glossy tresses which
it was to adorn without concealing, when
Maria, chancing to pass near them, observed
the pleased smile on the face of the young
lady, and the glance of satisfaction which
Lilian bestowed upon her handiwork; she
noticed, also, what no other eye had detected,
that a beautiful and costly bracelet, which
Miss C—— wore, had fallen from her arm,
and lay half hidden among the mass of flowers, ribbons, and lace, which were scattered
on the floor. Instantly her resolution was
taken; stooping down as if to replace the
disarranged goods in their boxes, she hastily
seized and secreted the ornament, then went
on deliberately with her self-imposed task,
until every flower was returned to its proper
place. Rising with the boxes on her arm,
she stepped up to Lilian, and, while asking
some trivial question, contrived, unseen by
mortal eye, to drop the bracelet into her
pocket.

Miss C——, quite unconscious of her loss,
and in very good humor with herself and all

3

the world beside, was soon driving rapidly toward home. Lilian, unsuspecting of the storm that was gathering around her, went calmly about her duties. Maria watched her anxiously, fearing she might discover the bracelet before her own wicked plot was fully matured, and, by her unaffected surprise at the discovery, defeat her purpose. Many a hasty glance she cast toward the window, hoping to see Miss C——'s carriage returning. Nor was it long before her wish was gratified. Miss C——, having missed the bracelet before leaving the carriage, returned immediately to the milliner's, feeling sure that it must be there.

She told Mrs. Pettigue of her loss, and strict search was made for the missing ornament, but it was nowhere to be found.

"Are you sure you wore the bracelet this morning, Miss C——?" inquired Mrs. Pettigue at last, sincerely hoping, for the credit of her establishment, that the cause of all this commotion would be found safe at home.

The doubt once raised, Miss C—— began to feel less certain that she had worn it. Indeed, it now seemed quite probable that she had not. Expressing regret for the trouble which she had given, she was about to leave the room, when Maria, who had taken no

part in the search, came to Mrs. Pettigue,
and with seeming reluctance said :

"I know Miss C—— had the bracelet on
her arm when she was here this morning, for
I noticed it particularly. I was on the other
side of the room when Lilian Ross was arranging the headdress. As Miss C——
raised her arm, I thought I saw the bracelet
fall. Just as I rose to go and pick it up,
Lilian stooped down and seemed to take
something from the floor. I concluded it
was the bracelet, and, supposing all was as it
should be, did not stop to see if she returned
it to Miss C——, but went on with my work
and thought no more about it."

This deliberate falsehood, though apparently intended for only Mrs. Pettigue's ear,
was not spoken in so low a tone but that both
Miss C—— and Lilian could distinctly hear
every word.

The flush of surprise and indignation
which suffused the fair face of the orphan
was readily mistaken for the blush of conscious guilt by those whose eyes were so
searchingly bent upon her.

Mrs. Pettigue sternly commanded her to
produce the bracelet, for that it was in her
possession there seemed but little doubt.

Lilian indignantly denied all knowledge

of it; but her changing color and faltering
voice were taken as evidence against her, and
every attempt that she made to defend herself from the cruel charge which was so unex-
pectedly made against her only increased her
trepidation and confirmed the suspicion of her
guilt. Finally, Mrs. Pettigue ordered that
she should be searched, when, to her terror
and amazement, and the triumph of her enemy, the bracelet was found in her pocket.
In vain she declared her innocence of the
theft, and her utter ignorance by what means
the ornament had become concealed about
her person. The words fell on ears that were
deaf to her pleading. Miss C—— clasped
the glittering band on her arm, and, not
deigning one glance at the pale, despairing
face of the young girl, she left the store, followed to the door by Mrs. Pettigue, who was
profuse in her expressions of regret that she
should have met with so much annoyance,
mingled with assurances that the culprit
should be instantly dismissed.

Returning, she summoned Lilian to her
private room, and, when her disgraced favorite stood alone before her, she gave free vent
to her wrath. Bitter, scornful words fell on
the ear of the orphan; fresh accusations were
heaped upon her, but she heeded them not;

she stood still and rigid as if turned to stone, the labored breath that parted her white lips the only evidence of life in the motionless figure.

When, Mrs. Pettigue's anger having exhausted itself, or rather exhausted her vocabulary of abuse, she placed in her hand the pittance which was her due, and bade her leave the house, never to enter it again, she obeyed mechanically; she knew but too well that any attempt to prove her innocence would be unavailing, and silently, with faltering steps, she passed into the street.

Alone, a stranger in the great city, the work which brought her and her little sister their daily bread snatched rudely from her hands, bearing the brand of a crime of which she was innocent, what wonder that despair took possession of her heart? The bright sunlight glared painfully on her glazed eyes; the many mingled sounds of busy life grated harshly on her ear; every face in the hurrying, eager throng seemed to her excited imagination to turn upon her looks of scorn and suspicion. She thought herself forsaken of heaven and condemned by earth. With a shuddering sense of utter desolation she hurried wildly on, until, guided more by instinct than reason, she gained her home. Then her overtasked strength gave way, and she fell insensible upon the floor.

The noonday sun, streaming in at the window, fell upon her colorless features, which even in unconsciousness wore a look of suffering and dismay; and the same bright rays rested upon the calm, upturned face of "little Faith," with her tempest-tossed garments.

CHAPTER V.

WHEN Lilian awoke from her long swoon, she was at first conscious only of a terrible throbbing pain in her temples, and a burning thirst; but suddenly the remembrance of all she had undergone since morning rushed upon her, and, starting to her feet, she clasped her hands to her aching brow, while with unsteady tread she paced the room. Once, as she neared the table, her eye caught the little statuette; she paused, and with a short, bitter laugh exclaimed, " Why was not I too formed of marble ? then I might smile so serenely under the lashings of the storm." But even while she spoke, a " still, small voice " whispered that her heart must be *softened*, not *hardened*, ere it could be moulded into a resemblance of the beautiful form before her. Oh ! when could she learn the lesson of faith ? The Heavenly Father had never yet forsaken her; still, whenever for a while the dark clouds enveloped her, she thought He had withdrawn

His smile. Because an erring mortal had treated her unjustly and cruelly, she had concluded the world was filled with nought but injustice and cruelty, even doubting the goodness of Him who marks the sparrow when it falls. And yet, was not the pretty image on which she gazed the memento of a kindly, generous, *human* heart, as well as a reminder that He who rules the tempest will not forsake those who trust in Him?

Slowly the bitter smile faded from the young girl's lips, and tears, which the strength of her agony had pressed back upon her full heart, fell in refreshing showers over her flushed cheek. She knelt by the little couch, and, with her head pillowed wearily on her folded arms, like a grieved child at its mother's knee, she murmured that beautiful prayer which He who was " a man of sorrows and acquainted with grief " left, a priceless legacy, to all the sorrowing children of earth. Still kneeling, then, with the sacred words yet upon her lips, Lilian fell asleep. Thus little Eva found her, when, nearly two hours later, she returned from school. The child was surprised that her sister was home so early, and frightened at her flushed, tear-stained face; and, after making one or two attempts to awake her, she ran and called Mrs. Havens,

LILIAN'S DARK HOUR.

who, in some alarm, hastened to the room, where she found her young tenant apparently suffering from a high fever. When aroused from her heavy slumber, Lilian was obliged to admit that she was really ill, and, with many tears, told Mrs. Havens the story of the lost bracelet.

The good lady was very indignant at the treatment she had received, and earnestly assured her of her entire belief in her innocence. This was a great comfort to poor Lilian, for she had, in her nervous excitement, imagined that Mrs. Havens would be unwilling to harbor in her house one who had been accused of theft, and unable to prove the accusation false. But she had misjudged her; for, though of a fretful, complaining disposition, and too much engrossed with her numerous cares to bestow much attention on those with whom the world seemed to be moving smoothly, she had still a kind heart and ready sympathy for sorrow and distress. She had always liked Lilian and would not turn from her at the first whisper of suspicion. In this, how different was the mother, whose unprepossessing exterior had at first made so unfavorable an impression upon her, from the daughter, whose more pleasing manners had won her regard!

3*

Mrs. Havens proved herself an excellent
nurse. She persuaded Lilian to go to bed,
bathed her head with cold water, and made
her take a cup of nice tea and a dainty slice
of toast, prepared by her own hands; and
only when her patient seemed more com-
posed, and gratefully assured her that she
was really much easier, did she consent to
leave her to attend to her own pressing duties. Even then she went with reluctance,
first charging Eva to be very watchful and
attentive to her sister, and to be sure to call
her if anything was wanted.

Little Eva had heard with indignation of
her sister's wrongs, and now, when she sat
quietly ensconced in the large rocking chair
with her doll and picture book, her thoughts
were busy with plans for proving Lilian's innocence and Maria's guilt (for that she had a
hand in the mystery the orphans as well as
Mrs. Havens had no doubt); and more angry,
revengeful thoughts crowded her little heart
than had found shelter there in all her short
life before. Alas! how widespread the dis-
astrous effects of sin! no human soul ever yet
yielded to temptation without injury to others.
Can a branch fall from the tree, and harm
only itself? See the torn leaves and scattered
blossoms of those that remain; and look how

the dust which arose as it struck the ground
has soiled the delicate petals of yonder little
violet.

Maria Roberts had never even seen little
Eva, and yet the shadow of her sin darkened
the pure spirit of the child. To be sure, Eva's
better nature soon shook off the baleful influence; but can such fierce passions as anger
and revenge enter the heart for the first time
and leave no trace behind ?   ●

The early winter twilight drew its sable
curtain around the sickroom, and the little
one, tired of her unusual stillness, grew sleepy,
and so, through force of habit, bethought her
of her evening prayer; but she was startled
by a new difficulty. How could she pray,
"Forgive us our trespasses as we forgive
those who trespass against us"? Did she forgive her unknown enemy as she would be
forgiven ? Should she leave the prayer un-
said this one night ? She grew afraid of the
darkness at the thought. What then—must
she forgive Maria Roberts? She had been
planning how she would go the next day and
accuse her before the whole shop of putting
the bracelet in Lilian's pocket, and how it
would all be then found out, and Maria
turned away in disgrace as Lilian had been;
and she had rejoiced as her imagination

painted the scene. Could she resign the revenge that lay within her grasp and looked
so tempting; or should she for the first time
lay her head upon a prayerless pillow? Not
long did the child hesitate between the good
and the evil that lay before her, but meekly
saying the prayer, and ceasing to wish for or
even think of revenge, she slept sweetly and
calmly.

CHAPTER VI.

THE following morning Lilian arose free from the pain and feverish excitement which had seemed to threaten a serious illness, but suffering from a feeling of prostration and debility almost as distressing. She moved listlessly about her morning duties, and, when Eva had gone to school, threw herself wearily on the lounge and lay there for hours, too languid even to think:

In the mean time, little Eva trudged bravely on her way in the clear, frosty morning. The few weeks of city life had added much to her stock of worldly wisdom, and she readily understood that Lilian's loss of employment deprived them of their only means of support; but she felt sure that their Heavenly Father would in some way provide for them. And as she walked briskly toward school, she formed many plans by which she might help her sister to earn their bread, all which plans seemed to her very promising, though in fact they were somewhat wild and impracticable. Occasionally a shade passed over her face as she remembered the origin of their trouble; but she would drive the thought away, quickening her pace as if to escape a danger.

When she reached school she was almost afraid to enter; it seemed as if they must all know that her sister was accused of stealing, and she ●t as if all eyes would be upon her. But the event which had brought distress upon their humble home was all unknown in the great world.

The day passed by unmarked, except that she was reproved for inattention to her lessons oftener than usual.

She walked home alone after school, for John and Jennie had found companions better suited to their taste; and she was not sorry to escape John's teasing and his sister's oppressive guardianship. Eva had never before been in the street alone. How she exulted in the sense of independence! Not one face in the thronging multitude had she ever seen before—she was like a tiny dewdrop, swallowed up and lost sight of in that restless sea of humanity; yet the child felt no fear. Her little foot touched the pavement with a firm, elastic tread, her bright eyes looking in at the shop windows as she passed, with admiring but not covetous gaze, upon the beautiful things which the merchants had spread out so temptingly. Finally she paused before a window in which were displayed ready-made garments for ladies' and children's wear. She was looking admiringly at an elegantly wrought baby dress, when her eye ·fell upon a card, on which was written, in large clear hand, " Wanted, a girl to do fine sewing. Inquire within. None but a first-rate seamstress need apply."

With some difficulty Eva deciphered the writing, and then stood for some moments in deep thought. At last her resolution was formed; slowly but unhesitatingly she entered the store. Once within the door, however, her courage deserted her, and she was quite at a loss for words to express her wishes.

Behind the counter were two or three girls, one of whom, seeing her embarrassment, accosted her with the inquiry:

" What will you have, sissy ? "

Thus forced to speak, Eva replied with a trembling voice:

" It says on the card in the window that you want some one to do fine sewing here, and—" But before she could finish the sentence, her questioner laughingly exclaimed:

"And you have come to offer your services." Then turning to her companions, she
continued: "Only think, girls; this young
lady proposes to fill the place Mary Davis
left last week!" A shout of laughter followed this announcement.

Poor little Eva, feeling very much morti-
fied and somewhat indignant, stood with
flushed cheeks and tearful eyes, wishing herself anywhere else, when an inner door suddenly opened, and a clear, mellow voice demanded in tones of surprise to know the
occasion of so much noise.

All were instantly silent, and when Eva
ventured to look up, a tall, rather fleshy lady,
in a rustling black-silk dress and snowy cap,
stood before her, listening to the stammered
apology of the young girl whose thoughtless
rudeness had produced the uproar. When
the latter had done speaking, the lady seated
herself, and, drawing Eva to her side, said
kindly:

"Now, my little girl, tell me what it was
you wished to say about my advertisement?
I do not suppose, as these foolish girls did,
that you meant to do the sewing with your
own little fingers, did you?"

"No, ma'am, indeed I did not," replied
the child, looking up into the benevolent face

which bent over her; "but my sister sews, oh! so beautifully, and—and I know she would like to come, and I thought perhaps you would take her."

"What makes you think your sister would wish to come; did she send you here?"

"Oh, no, ma'am; I only happened to see the card in the window; but she lost her place yesterday, and she feels very, very bad, because we don't have any money, only what she earns," said little Eva, with her tearful eyes fixed pleadingly on the lady's face.

"But, my dear child, I do not know that your sister could do my sewing. I am very particular about it, and must see a sample of her work before I can decide. If she really wishes the employment, perhaps she will come early to-morrow morning and bring some article that she has made."

"She made the apron I have on; I can show you that now," exclaimed the child; and, suiting the action to the words, she laid down her books and began hastily to unfasten her coat. The lady smiled, and there was a suppressed titter from behind the counter. Eva heeded it not; her outer garment was thrown aside, and the little apron triumphantly displayed. It was a simple gingham apron, but neatly and tastefully made.

Her new friend examined it critically, and then, turning to the eager, expectant child with an approving smile, she said, " I should like to see your sister. Tell her to come here in the morning, and, if she wishes the place, I think we can make an agreement."

Then, inquiring her own and her sister's name, she dismissed the happy child with a kiss.

There was no more stopping to look in at windows; even the great toyshop on the corner had no charm for Eva now. She almost flew on her way, and yet it seemed to her that she never moved so slowly, so impatient was she to reach home and tell Lilian the good news.

Lilian in the mean time was anxiously watching for the little adventurer. Jennie had returned at the usual time. She rather reluctantly admitted that she had left Eva to come alone, and Lilian, imagining some harm must have happened to her, as she was so long on the way, was on the point of going out to seek her, when the little girl bounded into the room, her cheeks flushed with exercise, and her eyes sparkling with excitement.

" Oh, sister Lillie ! " she exclaimed, " I have found the nicest lady in the world ; and she wants you to come and make the most beautiful little dresses and things that ever you saw ; and she thinks my apron—"

"Eva, Eva! what are you talking about ?" interrupted Lilian in bewilderment. "Where was the lady? what is it about 'beautiful little dresses,' and what has your apron to do with it all? Sit down here in your little chair, and talk more quietly, if you wish me to understand you." Thus checked, the child paused a moment to mentally untwist the tangled thread of her story, and then more coherently told of her exploit.

Lilian listened with surprise until she had finished the story ; then, catching her in her arms, declared she was the oddest little creature in the wide world, and questioned and cross-questioned her about the whole affair, and laughed at her having shown her apron. Whereupon Eva laughed too, and clapped her hands gleefully—not that she could perceive anything very amusing in her way of doing business, but she was delighted to see her sister cheerful once more. Then she made her promise that she would go with her the next morning and see the lady.

By the time all was arranged to her satisfaction, it began to grow dark, and Eva discovered it was almost tea time, and that she was very hungry. Away she sprang to set the table, while Lilian prepared their simple meal. The child went about her task singing softly to herself, and as she passed and re-passed before the stand on which was the image of Faith, the light cast a flickering shade on the face of the figure, and it seemed to her that " little Faith " was smiling upon her.

An hour or two later, Mrs. Havens and Lilian stood beside the bed, looking down upon the sleeping child. Lilian had been tell-ing of her little sister's adventure, and asking advice.

Mrs. Havens assured her she would do well to obtain the place if possible, for that the establishment had an excellent reputation. She was filled with admiration for little Eva, who had so soon found a way of escape from their difficulties, and now, as she looked upon the little sleeper, she raised her handkerchief to her eyes, with the whispered exclamation, " Dear child, dear child! only to think, it was the very first time she was ever in the street alone! Poor little thing, the cares of life have come upon her early." Ah! if good Mrs. Havens could have known what rosy dreams were floating about under those golden curls, she might have spared her tears and sympathy.

CHAPTER VII.

THE next morning being Saturday, there was no school, and Eva was to go and introduce Lilian to her new acquaintance. She was so excited as to be hardly able to eat her breakfast, and watched anxiously the suspicious-looking clouds which were drifting about in the wintry sky, for she had heard Mrs. Havens say to her sister, as she passed her in the hall, that she must not venture out if it stormed, as she was still far from well. But at last the sun shone out brightly. The rooms were put in the most perfect order, the last particle of dust wiped from the last chair, and Lilian having no longer any good excuse for delay, prepared herself and her little sister for their walk.

With very different feelings the orphans set out. Lilian dreaded to come again in contact with strangers; besides, she had some doubts as to the wisdom of following the guidance of such a child as Eva. Perhaps she had misunderstood the lady, or it might all have been intended as a joke upon the little girl, and she feared she might make herself appear ridiculous if she took it seriously. Not so Eva ; with the quick perception of childhood, she had read in the clear gray eyes and benevolent smile of her new friend sincerity of purpose and kindness of heart. And she bounded gladly onward, scarce able to make her impatient feet keep pace with her sister's slow step.

When they reached the store, what little courage Lilian had entirely forsook her. She would willingly have turned back, but before she could prevent it, Eva had entered the door, and she had no alternative but to follow.

One of the girls who had been so much amused at poor little Eva the day before, immediately ushered them into a small back room, where Mrs. Benton (for such was the name of Eva's friend) was ready to receive them. Her welcome was so kind, that Lilian lost in some measure the painful timidity with which she had entered, and was able to answer clearly and unhesitatingly the questions which were asked her.

Mrs. Benton examined and praised the work she had brought as a sample of her finest

sewing, and assured her she should be very
glad to give her employment, offering (much
to Lilian's surprise,) higher wages than Mrs.
Pettigue had given. She gladly accepted the
offer, and it was agreed that she should enter
Mrs. Benton's service on Monday morning.

With a lighter heart than she had known
for days, the young girl turned her steps
homeward. Eva skipped lightly at her side,
and was continually calling attention to the
wonderful sights which surrounded them.
The newly fallen snow gleamed pure and
white in the bright sunlight. Sleighs of
every graceful and fantastic form, with gay
trappings and merry bells, chased each other
through the streets, and the glad voices of the
riders rang blithely out above the city's busy
hum. The world looked bright and beautiful.
She forgot her own wrongs and sorrows in
sympathy with the seemingly universal joyousness. The clear frosty air gave new life
to her languid frame, and brought a health-
ful glow to her pale cheek. The dark clouds
of despondency and dread had for the time
rolled away, and her whole being revived in
the sunshine of hope.

Monday morning found Lilian early at
her post. Mrs. Benton, welcoming her with
a kind word and encouraging smile, led her

to a large cheerful room above the store, where several girls were already gathered around the fire, talking in subdued tones. At a table in the centre of the room stood a middle-aged woman busy cutting out and assorting work. There was something so peculiar in the appearance and manner of this latter person, that Lilian's attention was instantly attracted to her. She was rather below the medium height, and somewhat spare in person. Her hair, originally of a pale brown, was rendered still lighter by the many silver threads that time had added, till it was scarcely darker than the sallow brow above which it was so smoothly parted; the nose, much too large for the rest of the face, had an appearance of having been broken; her small, light blue eyes were fixed intently on the work before her; her fingers flew with the rapidity and almost the precision of machinery, while she sang, absent-mindedly, snatches of old songs, in a low, but singularly sweet voice.

Mrs. Benton, still followed by Lilian, stepped to her side, and laying her hand on her arm, said, "Miss Burr, here is Lilian Ross, the young girl I spoke to you about last evening."

She instantly dropped both muslin and

scissors, with which she was busied, and turning to Lilian, extended her hand and, with a smile which threw a gleam of beauty over the homely features, bade her welcome, in tones which, in speaking, lost little of the melody that had graced the lowly warbled song.

Mrs. Benton then left them, and Miss Burr, after asking a few friendly questions, explained to her the rules of the establishment, and the duties that would be required of her. Then stepping to a closet, she brought out a neat workbasket, containing needles, thread, scissors, &c. ; to this she tied a card, on which she wrote Lilian's name, and placed in it one of the parcels of prepared work that lay on the table before her. Handing it to her, she told her that it was for her use, and that she would be expected to keep it in order; then directing her to a seat near her own, she touched a little bell. Immediately all the girls took their seats, excepting two, who went to the closet, from which they brought several baskets similar to the one Lilian had received ; these they placed on the table, and, Miss Burr laying in each a piece of sewing, it was handed to the girl whose name it bore. Soon all were supplied, and with busy fingers they plied their needles.

4

Occasionally, Miss Burr passed through the industrious group, inspecting the work, and speaking to each a few kind words of praise or caution, as the case demanded. She watched the young stranger with evident interest, and seemed much pleased with her industry and the neatness of her needlework. Mrs. Benton, whose time was mostly occupied down stairs, came to the room several times during the day. Her gentle, yet dignified manner had won the confidence, as well as the respect of the little band, and Lilian could but contrast the smiles of pleasure which greeted her entrance, with the looks of dismay and confusion which always hailed Mrs. Pettigue's appearance in her work rooms. On the whole, she saw that she had made a pleasant exchange, and though her heart still throbbed with indignation, when she thought of the injustice from which she had suffered, she strove to forget the painful past, and think only of the many causes for thankfulness in the present.

CHAPTER VIII.

A LITTLE more than a week had passed since Lilian commenced her new employment, and all had gone prosperously with the orphans. To be sure, Eva found her trials rather on the increase. With Jennie, the novelty of having a younger child under her care, was beginning to pass away, consequently, she exercised a less strict guardianship over her, which fact, though it gave her more freedom, left her quite at the mercy of John, who never missed an opportunity to tease and annoy her. The poor child really feared him. He seemed to her so large and strong, she never doubted that he could perform all his threats; then he made such horrible faces when he chanced to meet her on the stairs, and would spring out at her from some hidden corner in the dark hall, with such a terrific whoop, that she grew almost afraid to leave the room when at home alone.

Once he came to make her a visit, as he said.   She received him as politely as possible, hoping to keep him in good humor; but he had promised himself rare sport, and was bound not to be disappointed. · He soon caught sight of a nice, tempting looking tart, which Lilian had left on the table for her little sister.   This he commanded the child to bring him.   She reluctantly obeyed, and he greedily devoured it all, stopping occasionally to exclaim tantalizingly, " Oh, how good ! " and to leer exultingly at his unwilling hostess. When the tart was gone, he placed his muddy feet in Eva's little chair, and catching up her doll, sat twirling it rapidly round and round by its arms until first one and then the other was torn off, then throwing poor mutilated Dolly across the room, he remained quiet, watching with glee the looks of distress with which the little girl examined its injuries; but Eva knew from experience that any show of grief on her part, far from causing him to regret his cruelty, would but add to what he called his fun, and increase his desire to tease; . so, suppressing her tears with a strong effort, she put the doll out of sight, quietly remarking, as if it had all been an accident, that she thought her sister could mend it.

This did not suit John; he had expected a

passion of anger and grief, and was prepared to enjoy her helpless rage, but now that her composure seemed likely to spoil his sport, he determined upon a more daring step, and seeing her favorite picture book near at hand, he deliberately placed it in the fire. Eva sprang to rescue it, but too late—a bright blaze for a moment cast its red light over her pale face and the malignant features of her tormentor, then died away, and a few white fleecy ashes was all that remained of the pretty pictures that had cheered so many lonely hours. She could endure no more, —even her fear of the cruel boy was lost in indignation. Turning her flashing eyes full upon him, she exclaimed:

"John Havens, you are a wicked, cowardly boy." The last adjective aroused all John's ire; raising his hand threateningly, he replied, angrily:

"How dare you say I am a coward, miss? You had better take it back, you little imp, or I'll shake you to pieces as I did your doll."

"I will not take it back," answered the undaunted child; "you *are* a coward. You would not dare to raise your finger to a boy of your own size, but because I am a helpless little girl, you are not afraid to do all you can to trouble me. Now," she continued, stretch-

ing her little hand toward the door with the
air of an empress, " leave the room, or I will
go directly down to your mother's dining-
room, and tell her before all at the table what
you have done."

The boy saw that she was in earnest, and
sullenly obeyed her command ; but from that
day he was more her enemy than ever, and,
as her dread of him returned with double
force when the excitement, which had for a
moment overmastered it, had subsided, he
found many an opportunity to annoy her.   ·

Eva, though not without her faults, was a
noble little thing. She knew that to com-
plain to Lilian would serve no good purpose,
and only make her unhappy ; so she kept the
trouble to herself, taking care to avoid John
as much as possible. Thus it happened that,
on the day with which this chapter opens, she
had contrived to linger at school until he and
his sister were on their way home, when she
followed alone. It was the day before Christmas, and Eva's happy little heart was full and
running over with joy and gladness. Not
that she expected a visit from St. Nicholas.
There are but few children, in this matter-of-
fact age, who have real faith in the jolly little
man with mouse-skins and reindeer, and our
little Eva was not of the number. She well

knew that it would require some outlay of her
sister's hard earnings to fill her stocking, and
had gravely announced several days previous
that she should not hang it up, for that Santa
Claus had already sent her a present—beautiful little Faith—which was quite enough for
a dozen Christmases, and that she was very
sure he could have nothing more for her this
year. And now, as she strolled slowly homeward, lingering with admiring gaze at the
windows of toy shops and confectioners, she
indulged no day-dream of possessing any of
the pretty things herself, yet, as I have already said, her heart was full of joy and gladness. The very sight of so much beauty was
enough to make her happy ; then to-morrow
would be a holiday for Lilian, as well as herself, and they could walk out together and see
all these wonders. At this thought she went
bounding merrily onward, determined to look
no more until her sister could share the
pleasure.

Presently she paused again, however.
She was before a church, from the broad
steps of which a man was busily sweeping an
uncommon litter ; he moved his broom most
energetically, keeping time to the merry tune
he whistled, never stopping to note how beautiful were the little twigs of pine and holly

that he so carelessly cast aside; but Eva's quick eye was charmed by the effect of green leaves and red berries against the white snow. For a moment she stood looking on with a pleased smile; then came a feeling of regret as she thought how soon it would all be trampled under foot and destroyed. Stepping forward as the man's broom flirted off a larger and handsomer sprig than the others, she picked it up, and, raising her eyes to his face, asked timidly, "May I have this, please?"

With a good-natured laugh he replied, "Of course you may, sissy, and as much more as you want; it is only the litter that's left from trimming the church."

The child, thanking him for the permission, immediately busied herself in gathering the pretty green twigs which he seemed so much to despise. The amused sexton watched her for a while, and then exclaimed:

"I say, sis, what are you going to do with all that rubbish, any way?"

"It isn't rubbish!" replied Eva, indignantly, "but beautiful evergreens, and I'm going to dress our room for Christmas, so that it will look bright and cheerful when my sister is home."

"Well, that is a good idea; but it ain't worth while for you to be freezing your fingers picking up any more of those. Come here, and I'll give you something that'll do better."

Eva followed him into the vestibule of the church; there in a corner stood a large basket.

" See here, little one," he said; " I was awfully provoked when I found there was all this left, and that I had got to see to carrying it away; but ' it is an ill wind that blows no good,' and now you shall have the very prettiest bunches there are here to dress up your parlor with. And look here, sis," he continued, with a merry twinkle in his small, bright eyes, " you had better just step in the church, and see how it's done; perhaps you'd like to follow the pattern."

. The little girl pushed the door as he directed; it opened easily to her touch, and as quickly closed after her. She was alone in the church, and a feeling of awe, but not of fear, crept over her as she looked around. The last rays of the setting sun stole through the painted windows, casting a subdued yet varied light over the massive pillars and lofty arches of the edifice; and, clinging round the cold, hard stone, in graceful garlands, the pine, the cedar, and holly had met together to beautify the sanctuary in honor of His

4*

birth, who came to bring life and immortality to light.

Little Eva stood still, wrapt in holy thoughts and filled with unutterable admiration, when suddenly the door was thrown open, and the jolly sexton exclaimed :

"Well, sissy, do you think you can make yours look anything like that ? "

"Like that ? oh, no, surely the angels must have done it ! " cried the enthusiastic little lover of beauty.

"Humph ! " ejaculated her companion, with a shrug of his shoulders, "well, I was around most of the time it was being done, and I can't say that I saw any angels, but maybe it was because I didn't have my specs on."

The child heeded not his reply, but, thanking him in low but grateful tones for the beautiful greens he had selected for her, she cast one more look back upon the church, and then hastened toward home with her prize.

She was so fortunate as to reach their own room without encountering John ; and, barring the door against all intruders, set busily to work with her festive preparations. And no light task she found it to carry out her plan ; such a tearing of her little hands with the holly, such a climbing on chairs and tables, such a stretching of her chubby arms, in vain efforts to hang wreaths in impossible places; now searching for a lost pin, now reconstructing a garland, which the breaking of an unlucky thread had spoiled; but she toiled patiently on, and at last had the satisfaction of seeing her simple decorations completed, though not until the short winter twilight had given place to gaslight. The little room looked very pretty in its Christmas dress, and Eva grew impatient for her sister's return, that she might show her handiwork; but Lilian was later than usual, and at last she concluded to go down and watch for her through the side lights of the front door. Throwing her little cloak around her, she stole cautiously out into the hall, and, after peering anxiously into the gathering darkness, and listening a moment to make sure that John was not lurking near, she locked the door behind her, and, creeping as silently as possible down the stairs, was soon standing with her face pressed close to the narrow strip of glass, watching eagerly every form that came within her small field of vision.

Rapidly the pedestrians hurried by, each with bundles or overflowing baskets, that told of a good time coming to-morrow. Even the poor washerwoman, who lived round the corner, as she stopped under the street light to arrange more securely the contents of her market basket, revealed the head of a tin horse and the wheel of a toy wagon, and Eva was glad to know that her little red-haired boys were to have a merry Christmas. Still Lilian did not come, and the weary little watcher had begun to feel very disconsolate at the delay, when a long, light wagon drove up to the door. She could see by the gaslight the word "Express" printed in gilt letters on its side. A man sprang from it, and, running up the steps, gave the bell a quick, hurried pull. Eva opened the door, thinking he would inquire for Mrs. Havens, or perhaps some of her boarders; but, to her surprise, he asked if Miss Lilian Ross lived there.

The wondering child answered in the affirmative, adding the gratuitous information that she was her sister.

"Then, little one," he replied, with a smile, "perhaps you can tell me what to do with the box I've got here for her." So saying, he returned to the wagon and lifted out a square box, which Eva thought, from the way he carried it, must be heavy. He followed her up the stairs, and, placing his burden on the floor in their room, hastened away. Eva was still examining the outside of the myste-

rious box when Lilian returned. She looked
around with surprise at the transformation
which had taken place in her humble home.
The glossy leaves and shining berries, gleam-
ing brightly in the gaslight, gave the room
such a festive air that she hardly recognized
it, and would surely have thought she was in
the wrong house, but that Eva sprang to her
side rattling off a torrent of explanations,
which, though at first adding confusion to
doubt, finally convinced her that the excited
child was herself the author of the wreaths
and garlands, and that the only mystery in
the case was still shut up in the box.

Eva' was soon dispatched to borrow a
hammer of Mrs. Havens, when Lilian, stepping to the bureau, carefully secreted in one
of the drawers a small parcel which she had
kept hidden under her shawl.

Little Eva almost flew on her errand, not
even stopping to make sure of John's absence
as she ran through the dark passages. She
found Mrs. Havens in a state of more than
usual worry and excitement, striving hope-
lessly to impress upon a new recruit from the
Emerald Isle the importance of setting the
tea-table before she made the toast. The
little girl was somewhat abashed at the
sharply uttered " Run away, child, and keep

out of the muss!" which greeted her entrance into the stormy kitchen; still she ventured, while standing as near the door as
possible, to ask for the hammer, and explain
for what they wished to use it.

Mrs. Havens, somewhat mollified by her
timid manner, and perhaps feeling some
regret that her hasty words had cast a
damper upon the child's happiness, gave her
what she desired, with a grim attempt at a
smile; and she bounded away to her own
more cheerful quarters, where Lilian was
patiently awaiting her return. With some
expenditure of strength and exercise of me-
chanical skill, the box was at last forced
open, and its contents subjected to their eager
inspection. There was a fine large turkey,
all ready roasted, there were mince pies,
apple pies, and pumpkin pies, a large loaf of
cake, and a small pot of jelly. Then there
was a little pasteboard box, containing stockings and mittens, a very pretty needle book
for Lilian, and a pin cushion for Eva, with
the words "Remember me" formed in pins
on one side, and last, though not least, a
letter from good Aunty Smith, begging her
"dear children" to accept the "humble
Christmas offering." The mittens and stockings were of her own knitting; the needle

book and cushion were from Miss Becky,
who assured them they were made after an
entirely new and much approved pattern.
Each had had a share in preparing the eata-
bles, and they both asked that their young
friends would think of them and the old
home while enjoying their Christmas dinner.
Then followed a summary of all the village
news, a particular account of Ponto, Puss,
and the chickens, and many other items of
household gossip, which were of absorbing
interest to the orphans.

It was later than usual ere little Eva was
ready for bed that night. When she had
said her prayers, she raised her rose-bud lips
for a good-night kiss, and Lilian, as she gave
it, asked :

" Why, Birdie, ar'n't you going to hang
up your stocking? don't you know this is
Christmas Eve ? "

The child understood the meaning smile
with which her sister spoke, and, catching up
her stocking with delighted surprise, pinned
it to the mantelpiece ; then springing into
bed, she soon fell asleep, wondering what it
could be that Lilian had for her, hoping she
had not deprived herself of anything to
gratify her.

When satisfied that her little sister was
sleeping, Lilian took out the parcel that she

had placed in the bureau, and, unrolling it,
brought to light a small doll and a piece of
blue silk—the latter a contribution from Miss
Burr; then, taking from her workbasket a
roll of white cambric and a few bits of lace,
she seated herself in the rocking chair by the
table, and soon her willing fingers were engaged in fashioning the most fairylike garments imaginable; and so swiftly flew the
bright little needle that ere long Dolly's
tasteful outfit was completed. " All but the
shoes," said Lilian, as she held it up to take a
critical survey of her work; " Birdie would
not be quite satisfied if I left it barefooted,
though she would not say a word, I know,
dear little thing !" Thus soliloquizing, she
again opened the bureau drawer, and after a
moment's search found an old kid glove, out
of which she skilfully formed a very neat pair
of little shoes, which proved a most excellent
fit. And now the last bow was tied and the
work of love finished. Taking from her
pocket a little package of candy, she put it
first into the stocking; then carefully smoothing Dolly's fine dress, placed her with her
head peeping out at the top, and, turning
away with a smile of satisfaction, she sought
her pillow.

The morning sun, streaming through frost-
covered windows, shone upon a happy scene

in that little room. The Christmas garlands looked fresh and green in the cheerful light; the breakfast table was neatly spread. Lilian was busily engaged preparing some little extra dish for the meal, occasionally looking up from her task to speak a loving word to Eva, who was dancing about the room for very joyousness, with her new doll in her arms. On the whole, it was a merry Christmas day for the orphans, though sometimes a shade of sadness would cross Lilian's brow, as she contrasted it with the days that were past.

They took a long walk through the gay streets, as Eva had anticipated, and came home with sharpened appetite to the beautiful dinner which awaited them.

Mrs. Havens had kindly allowed them the use of her oven to warm the turkey, as their own was much too small to accommodate it. When all was ready, they sat down to a banquet which Eva declared was fit for a king.

Ah! what a delightful home flavor had all the dainties, and how lovingly the sisters spoke of the dear friends whose affection had prepared this treat for them.

We will leave our young friends seated at the window, with its holly-decked curtains, watching the sunset of this bright day, and pass over many months before we again resume the thread of simple history.

CHAPTER IX.

WINTER gave place to spring, and spring brightened into summer, and all went well. Lilian gained daily more and more the esteem and confidence of her employer. Eva made rapid progress in her studies, and, as John, finding there was but little " fun " in teasing one who bore his tyranny so uncomplainingly, now but seldom molested her, she was as happy as the day was long. Sometimes, indeed, she longed for the green fields and shady groves among which all the previous summers of her short life had been spent, and she wondered how it fared with her little garden at B——, and whether the honeysuckle and rose vines were doing well this year, and wished she might hear the robins sing in the apple tree once more; but she said nothing of all these vain yearnings to Lilian, but sought to make herself what amends were in her power by frequent visits to the park. She was delighted to find that birds made their nests in the trees there, and decided that the fountain, when it played, was a very good substitute for the brook. And as she had now become quite familiar with the city streets, she would often stroll into the up-town avenues to see the beautiful flowers that decked the parterres before the mansions of wealth. No feeling of envy detracted from the delight with which she watched the gradual unfolding of these floral gems, and perhaps they were the source of greater delight to her than to those who owned them.

Thus, with cheerfully performed duties and simple pleasures, time passed rapidly on, till now the leaves in the park are growing brown and sear; the summer flowers have given place to the more hardy asters and dahlias; the shortened days and an occasional chilly blast tell the approach of autumn, that gaudy herald of dreary winter. But there are heavier tidings afloat than those which murmuring nature whispers to the birds; and, as the rumor passes from lip to lip, manly cheeks blanch and stout hearts quail. A harvest of unusual abundance has been gathered into overflowing barns, and yet the words "want and distress" are stammered by every tongue. A great financial crisis has suddenly broken upon the country, and the shock, as of electricity, passes through every department of the moneyed world. Yes! so intimately are the interests of mankind interwoven, that the laborer in his garret, and the millionnaire by his fireside, alike feel and shudder at the fearful vibration.

As weeks pass on the gloom increases; crash follows crash, as princely fortunes crumble to the dust, burying many a humble hearthstone in the ruins. The streets are thronged with men, women, and children, thrown out of employment, vainly seeking the means to earn a scanty meal. The hearts of men grow tender and compassionate amid such general distress, and the gentle voice of charity, too often stifled by the shouts of prosperity, is heard calling upon all such as will, to " come and buy bread without money and without price." Many employers, careful rather of the interests of their employees than their own, struggle bravely on, refusing to stop their work while there is a possibility of paying the workman's hire. Of this class was Mrs. Benton. Though her business was seriously affected from the very beginning of the panic, she would not dismiss any of the hands; but when she found her-

self obliged to retrench in some way, she
called them together, and, briefly explaining
her situation, told them that, as she was resolved not to cast any of them off so long as
it was in her power to avoid it, she was com-
pelled to reduce the wages of all. To this
the girls consented uncomplainingly, but with
heavy hearts, for well they knew that Mrs.
Benton would not take such a step unless the
necessity was great.   .

After this all went on much as usual for a
few weeks; but Lilian, who, though she
dared not question, watched Mrs. Benton's
countenance anxiously, saw the shadow of
care and perplexity deepen day by day upon
her brow. Those were gloomy days to the
young girl, in which she watched the gathering of the storm which she knew must burst
upon her. If at home she chanced to encounter Mrs. Havens, the look of absolute despair,
which had taken the place of her usual expression of discontent, fairly frightened her.
In the workroom, the girls talked in low
tones of acquaintances who had lost their
situations, and how impossible it was for
them to procure other employment, until she
grew sick at heart, for all of these had some
staff, however weak, upon which to lean till
the dark hour had passed; but to what could

she look when the power to help herself
should be taken away?

This weight of care, so unsuited to her
years, soon showed its effects upon her health.
She grew pale and thin; her step lost its
elasticity, her eye burned with an unnatural
lustre, she started nervously at every sudden
sound or movement. The nights, instead of
bringing refreshing repose, were spent in
feverish tossings and wild speculations as to
the future. At last the dread which had
been sapping her life became a reality. It
was Saturday night, and Mrs. Benton came
into the room as usual to pay the girls their
week's wages. There was something in her
manner which riveted the attention of all,
and filled poor Lilian with consternation.
Silently she handed to each the amount that
was due them, and then, turning sadly to the
expectant group, she said that the event
which for weeks she had foreseen and struggled against had at last overtaken her; she
had failed, and the next week her stock would
be sold at auction for the benefit of creditors.
As it was no longer in her power to supply
them with the work which they so much
needed, she could but bid them go forth,
trusting in Providence, and pray that He
would prosper them in some other under
taking.

Many tears were shed at the cheerless parting, but to Lilian came no such relief. With dry, burning eyes, she received and responded to the affectionate farewell of Mrs. Benton and Miss Burr, then turned with languid step toward home.

Little Eva was watching for her return, eager to tell how she had gone up to the head of her class for spelling a hard word that all the large girls missed; but at sight of her sister's pale, despairing face, the child forgot her own triumph, and entreated to know what had grieved her.

Lilian took her on her lap, and in measured tones, whose unnatural calmness frightened her more than the words themselves, told her of the calamity that had befallen them. Eva's tears flowed fast. Too well she knew that this new misfortune could not be so easily remedied as others which had clouded their path; for she had heard on all sides of the hard times, and how people were suffering from want who were ready and willing to work if work could but be found, yet it was only for a moment that her faith faltered. Throwing her arms around Lilian's neck, she exclaimed, "Don't cry, Lillie! God has always taken care of us, and I know He will now."

But the hopeful words met with no response in her sister's breast. With a hasty kiss, she turned from the little would-be comforter, and gave herself up to her own foreboding thoughts.

In all the dark horizon there was but one streak of light—the remembrance of her old home. She could take her little sister and go back to dear, good Aunty Smith. She knew how gladly she would give them shelter; and surely they had friends enough in their native village who would supply them with bread, if need be, until better days. Her pride shrank from the thought of returning to B—— to live on charity; but her aching heart longed for the sympathy and protection which she was sure there awaited her. It would be so soothing to pour out her sorrows on the gentle breast of her old friend, and to hear Miss Becky's cheerful voice once more, as she busied herself with her household duties. She knew that the money she had received that evening was more than enough to pay Mrs. Havens her due and defray the expenses of the journey, and determined to leave as soon as she could write and inform their friends of their coming. The moment this resolve was taken, the heavy cloud was lifted which had seemed crushing her to the earth, and hope seemed smiling upon her from its lessening gloom.• Calling Eva to her side, she was about to tell her of her decision, well knowing how delighted she would be at the prospect of going "home," when a rap at the door interrupted her.

"Two cents! the man's waiting," exclaimed the querulous voice of Mrs. Havens' overtasked maid-of-all-work, as she thrust a letter into Eva's hand.

Ah, that letter! how eagerly Lilian caught it from her little sister, confident that in some way it would help them out of the difficulties which surrounded them. How excited Eva was at so unexpected an event as a letter for them! so very much flurried, indeed, that she twice dropped the all-important pennies while taking them across the room to Bridget, thereby quite exhausting that damsel's slender stock of patience.

With a light step and a joyous heart the child sprang back to her sister's side; but alas! the momentary sunshine had fled. With colorless face, and a wild, startled look in her beautiful eyes, she was gazing upon the yet unopened letter, and now, for the first time, Eva saw that it was sealed with black. Tremblingly Lilian broke the ominous seal, and read the confirmation of her worst fears.

5

The letter was from Miss Becky, and contained the sad announcement of her mother's death. The good old lady, after a short illness, had closed her eyes forever upon the world, as calmly as an infant falls asleep on its mother's bosom ; and the sorrowing daughter, writing to the young orphans, who she knew would share her affliction, endeavored to convey to them a share also of her consolation, by dwelling on the peaceful departure of their loved one, and the joys by which she was now surrounded, in which they too might hope to participate when life's short trial should be passed. In a postscript Miss Becky informed them that her brother, who had come from the far West to see his mother's form laid in its last resting place, had proposed that she should return with him and henceforth make his home her own. She had accepted the kind proffer, had already found new occupants for the cottage, and, ere this letter reached her young friends, would be far on her way toward her new home.

Lilian read it all with a faltering voice and streaming eyes, while Eva gave vent to her grief in sobs and tears. The little tea table was not spread that night ; the orphan sisters were too absorbed in their new sorrow to feel aught of hunger. Eva, lying on the lounge, had cried herself to sleep ; and Lilian, seated beside her, with her hands folded languidly in her lap, heeded not the gathering darkness, for once more the deeper darkness of despair had closed around her.

CHAPTER X.

One day, shortly after Lilian had left Mrs. Benton, she was seated by the fire making a bonnet for Eva's doll. Her heart was not in the work; she would gladly have thrown aside the gay-colored silk, that, with its brightness, mocked her distress, but her little sister stood by her side watching with glee the construction of Miss Dolly's new hat. There was sorrow enough in store for the light-hearted child, she feared, and she would not deprive her of one pleasure which it was in her power to bestow; so with forced cheerfulness she pursued her task, replying patiently to the little one's numberless questions. But Eva was neither so careless nor so thoughtless as she seemed. She was pleased with her new toy, and watched with delight its points of beauty as they gradually formed beneath her sister's skilful fingers;

yet, as we shall see, her pleasure had a deeper
source than the mere selfish gratification of
the moment. She well understood the difficulties of their situation. She had seen how
little there was left in the purse when Lilian
paid Mrs. Havens the rent that morning.
She knew that the coal was almost gone, and
she also knew that, live as economically as
they might, it must cost them something for
food each day. How long, then, would the
little store last, and what could they do when
it was spent? These momentous questions
had busied her thoughts for some time. One
thing was certain, she thought: it would be
worse than useless for Lilian to seek employment at present, and consequently it seemed
to her equally certain that she must do something herself to raise the needed funds. Satisfied with this decision, and wearied with so
much silent cogitation, she dismissed the
whole subject from her mind for the time
being, leaving the ways and means of accom-
plishing her object for future meditation, and,
remembering that Dolly's head gear was in a
sadly dilapidated condition, she had hunted
up a box containing the numerous scraps of
silk and bits of ribbons which kind-hearted
Miss Burr had from time to time given her,
and had coaxed Lilian to redeem her forgot-

ten promise to make it a new bonnet. Now, as she watched the progress of her work, a thought struck her which made her heart beat fast, and sent bright, hopeful sparkles into her blue eyes.

"Sister Lillie," she asked eagerly, "couldn't you make ever so many little hats like that?"

"I suppose I could, pet," replied Lilian, with a faint smile; "but is not one enough at a time?"

"Yes, enough for me, Lillie; but don't you know I could sell them and get some money? then you need not look so sorry all the while, and the good times would come back again, and oh, it would be so nice!" exclaimed the child, fairly dancing about the room with delight, as she fancied she had at last found the path that should lead them out of their labyrinth of troubles. Then, springing back to her sister's side, she wound her plump arms around her neck, saying coaxingly, "You will make them, won't you, Lillie?"

"I would do anything to give you pleasure, Birdie, but fear if I should do as you wish it would only bring you disappointment. Who do you think would buy the things when they were made?"

"I don't know *who* would buy them, but I

am sure somebody would. I could take them
in a little basket, and ask the people as they
passed along the street."

"Never, Eva!" exclaimed the elder sister, catching the child to her heart, as if to
shield her from some threatened danger;
"never shall you go wandering through the
streets like the miserable little children we
have so often seen in this great, dreary city,
striving all day long to gather together a few
pennies, and receiving angry words and scornful looks instead. No, darling, it shall not
come to that; I will work my fingers to the
bone first!" and, covering her little sister
with kisses, the agitated girl burst into a passion of tears. Alas! it needed but a moment's thought to remind her how impossible
it would be to make good her last words; for
where could she procure the work which she
would so gladly undertake? Eva, though
surprised and distressed at the effect of her
artless proposal, was still unwilling to aban-
don the plan, and, as soon as Lilian was calm
enough to listen, she renewed her persuasions,
and was finally so far successful as to gain
her reluctant consent to make a number of
little hats and other fancy articles, and allow
her to take them to the nearest toyshop and
try to sell them.

Now work commenced in earnest. Eva, full of expectation, confident of success, and anxious to help, rummaged every nook and corner in search of pasteboard and whatever other necessary and unnecessary material she happened to think of, emptying drawers and boxes in her eagerness, without even thinking of replacing their contents, until the usually neat room presented a scene of confusion that would have driven any thrifty housewife distracted. Then, suddenly perceiving the mischief she had done, she set about repairing it, though with somewhat abated ardor, it must be confessed.

Lilian, in the mean time, scarcely heeding the little girl's movements, had been busily plying her needle, so that by the time Eva had restored things to order, she was putting the finishing touches to another doll's bonnet, and even began to feel some interest in her employment. Eva, perceiving how little good had resulted from her own unaided efforts, now begged her sister to tell her what she could do to help, and very readily learned, with the aid of patterns which she prepared for her, to cut out pasteboard frames for baskets and boxes ; each piece of pasteboard Lilian covered with silk, and when the corresponding pieces were neatly sewed together, they formed very tasteful little affairs. Eva was delighted, and considered their fortune already made; and even Lilian's smile was less sad than it had been of late.

All that day and the next the orphans busied themselves with their pleasing employment. On the third morning it was agreed that Eva should try to dispose of the articles that were finished, at the toy merchant's. Lilian arranged their small stock in trade in the basket so as to show to the best advantage, and Eva, as she raised the cover to take a last peep, was sure no one could resist the temptation to buy. Besides an assortment of tiny bonnets that might have turned the head of any belle in Fairy-land, there were two beautiful little chairs, and quite a variety of workboxes and baskets.

The child, carefully wrapped up in her little cloak, with the basket on her arm, trudged bravely along, caring not for the cold, nor heeding the dull, gray clouds that covered all the sky, and occasionally sent a few snow flakes whirling slowly through the air. Her heart was so full of hope and faith that the cheerless morning seemed beautiful to her. Not so with Lilian, who watched her from the window. She had no confidence in

the success of their experiment, and had engaged in it only to please the child, and to
while away some of the unemployed hours
which dragged so heavily by; and now, as
she stood gazing after the little black-robed
figure that hurried along the street with such
a springing tread, she sighed, for she doubted
not that the child, with all her bright expect-
ations, was hastening to meet a sad disappointment. *She* saw the leaden clouds, which like
a pall shut out the sunlight, and shuddered
as she marked the feathery harbingers of winter storms which fell so silently to the earth;
then, turning to the bureau drawer, she
opened her purse and counted over, for the
twentieth time, the few pieces of silver that
remained of her little hoard, saying to herself,
in a terrified whisper, "What will become
of us when this is gone?"

In the mean time Eva had reached the
toyshop. Her heart beat very fast as she
with some difficulty raised her basket to the
counter, and in a faltering voice asked the
stern-looking man who stood behind it to buy ·
her toys.

"No, child, no!" he answered angrily;
"I can't sell what I've got here already, to
say nothing of such trumpery as that," and
he pushed the basket impatiently toward her.

The little girl hastened from the store; she was frightened by the harsh words and rough manner of the man, and for a moment felt very much like crying, but, brushing away the tears, she said to herself, " Suppose one man is cross—that's no reason why all should be. I'll try again." Recollecting that there was another toyshop a few blocks off, she turned her steps in that direction and hurried onward. Arriving at the store with the unkind words still ringing in her ears, she felt very loth to go in, and lingered at the door, half inclined to turn about and go home; but, remembering her sister's sad face, which she had hoped to brighten, she summoned her failing courage and entered.

Behind the counter was seated a pleasant-looking woman, busily engaged sewing. She rose with a smile when the door opened, evidently expecting a customer; but, though the smile faded as Eva made known her errand, it gave place to a pitying look that was as kind. She examined the contents of the basket, while the child told her simple story, and then said, in tones of real regret, " I am sorry I cannot buy any of these beautiful things to-day, my little girl; but these are hard times, dear—I hardly sell anything nowadays." Then, seeing the look of disappointment with

which the child took up the basket, she
added encouragingly, "You had better offer
them to the ladies you pass in the street. I
am sure they would buy them, for the sake
of this sweet face;" and she stroked Eva's
clustering curls with her broad, plump hand.

The little girl turned toward home with
lingering steps. She longed to go farther,
feeling quite sure that she should meet with
better fortune the next time; but she knew
Lilian would be anxious if she was long ab-
sent, and she had already been farther than
she intended. She was sorely tempted to
follow the advice of the good woman at the
toyshop, and ask some of the gaily-dressed
ladies she met to buy her goods; but this
Lilian had forbidden, and she must not diso-
bey her "mother-sister."

CHAPTER XI.

SEVERAL days had passed since Eva's un-
successful attempt at trade. The winter had
really come now ; snow lay glittering on the
ground, and Lilian had been obliged to buy
more coal, which very much lightened her
already light purse. It was a bitter cold
morning. The orphans had eaten nothing
since noon of the previous day. Lilian sat
with her head bowed on one hand, gazing
wistfully upon the solitary dime which she
held in the other. It was the last of her little
hoard, and Eva, wrapped in cloak and hood,
stood before her, ready to go out and exchange it for the bread they so much needed.
The child guessed what gloomy forebodings
cast their shadow over her sister's brow as
she looked at the little coin, and thought it a
favorable moment to again urge her plan of
relief. Going quickly to the closet, she re-

turned with the basket, from which they had not yet removed the pretty toys on which her hopes still rested. "Sister Lillie," she said pleadingly, " mayn't I try to sell these now ? "

" You have tried, child."

" Yes; but I mean, can I take them and go and sit on some steps in Broadway where the people can see them ? and then, when they stop to look, I can tell how much we need the money, and I am sure somebody would· buy. Please let me go, Lillie."

" Get the bread first, dear," Lilian replied, in a low, trembling voice. Eva needed no second bidding. Glad of the implied consent which her sister had given to her request, and urged on by her own keen appetite, she almost flew to the nearest bakery, and soon returned with the loaf which was to supply them with breakfast, dinner, and supper.

Lilian cut the small portion which must satisfy their present want, and the young sisters ate their scanty meal in silence. Lilian grew sick at heart as she thought of her petted darling encountering all the hardships and abuse which she imagined must be the inevitable lot of the little street merchants, whom she had so often looked upon with pity, without dreaming that her own little Eva would ever share their experience; but there seemed no other hope, and she dared not longer refuse the child's entreaty.

Brave little Eva felt no fear, and, when Lilian had given her a parting kiss, and many injunctions to be careful in crossing the streets, and, above all, to be sure to come home if anything troubled her, she took her basket on her arm, and trudged off to seek her fortune, as she said.

She had decided to take her stand somewhere in Broadway, but, as she walked down that gay thoroughfare, she was somewhat at a loss what spot to choose, until, coming to St. Paul's churchyard, her attention was attracted by an old blind organ grinder who had stationed himself there, and, with his benumbed fingers, was perseveringly turning the crank of his instrument, though the music that he thus set free was drowned by the countless harsher sounds which filled the air. His face wore a sad yet patient expression, and his long, white beard gave him a very venerable look. Not far from him, seated on the stone work which supported the iron fence before the church, was a black woman, who, notwithstanding the biting coldness of the morning, was knitting as industriously as if she was sitting at her own fireside. By her side was a little stand, cov-

ered with apples and oranges. Seeing Eva
stop and look toward her, the woman pointed
to her fruit: " Buy some apples or a nice
orange, little miss ? " she asked, with a good-
natured smile.

The child hesitated a moment, then stepping close to her side, she said, half timidly,
half confidingly :

" I have no money to buy anything, but I
have some little things in my basket that I
want to sell. May I sit by you and try if
any one will buy them ? "

The woman seemed surprised, and glanced
inquiringly at Eva, as if she wondered that a
little girl so nicely dressed and evidently so
well cared for should be out so cold a morning on such an errand. Then, apparently
concluding that it was only a plan of the
child's to gain more pocket money for herself
than she was allowed to have, and that she
was probably out without leave, she said,
rather coldly :

" I tink, miss, dat you had better go
home, and leave sech work for poor chil'en."

Eva saw the change in her manner, and
guessed the cause.

" Indeed," she exclaimed, " we *are* very
poor ; we have only part of a loaf of bread at
home, and not a cent of money. My sister

cannot get any work, and I don't know what we shall do if I can't sell these."

The woman was used to the study of human nature, and readily saw that the child spoke the truth. By means of a few kindly put questions, she induced her to tell enough of her own and her sister's past history to enlist all the sympathies of her warm, honest heart in their behalf. Many a time in this world is it found to be true that those who are most willing to help the struggling poor are they who themselves know the bitterness of poverty; so in this case the little orphan found a much needed friend in the poor negro woman, who earned her own scanty living in the same way as that to which she looked with so much hopefulness; and *she* proved herself not only a friend in need, but a friend indeed. She selected the sunniest place for her little protégée, and helped her to arrange her wares in the most attractive manner on the stone coping which was to serve her as both counter and seat. Then, bidding her " keep a good heart," she left her, and went back to her own neglected stall just in time to see two chubby school boys, who were her daily customers, pass on with a disappointed air, evidently wondering that she was not in her accustomed place, ready to serve them with her luscious fruit. The poor woman sighed, for her daily income was small, and these boys were very desirable patrons, with their endless supply of half-dimes and pennies, and their insatiable appetite for apples and oranges. But that she felt no ill will for the little girl who had been the innocent cause of her loss, was evident not only from the kindly glances which she cast toward her, but also from the fact that she presently rose, selected the largest and ruddiest apple on her table, and, hastening to where Eva sat anxiously watching the passers-by, placed it in her hand, and, with a smile and a nod, hurried back to her own seat without waiting for thanks. Oh, how eagerly little Eva devoured the rosy apple! She had tried to fancy that the morning's meagre breakfast was a very hearty meal, and that she should not be hungry again all day; but her walk in the sharp, frosty air had added keenness to her half-satisfied appetite, and she was beginning to feel sick with hunger, when this new but true friend placed the fruit in her hand.

Eva had just finished the apple, and was looking earnestly toward the black woman's stand, striving to catch her eye, that she might smile back her thanks, when two ladies stopped suddenly before her, one of them exclaiming to the other, " Look, sister, one of these little hats would be the very thing for Bessie's new doll."   The lady thus appealed to took from a paper parcel in her hand a china doll's head, and began trying on to it first one and then another of the dainty little bonnets which formed so important a part of the young adventurer's stock in trade.   One was too small, another too large, and the color of a third did not suit.   How anxiously Eva watched them ! how dishearteningly each objection fell upon her quick ears, and what a great bound her heart gave, when at last her fastidious customers hit upon one which they pronounced " just right " ! For a moment she could scarce gain self-possession enough to tell the price, and for many moments after the ladies had passed on she sat looking at the two shining little bits of silver that lay in her hand, while tears of joy sparkled in her bright blue eyes.   She longed to run home and show Lilian this first fruit of their united labor—but that was impossible ; so at last she put the money into her little empty purse, and, with renewed hope and faith, sat patiently waiting for more customers.

Presently an old lady stopped and looked over her little stock of goods, but evidently without much satisfaction.

"Haven't you got any needle-books?" she said, turning sharply toward Eva.

"No, ma'am—I'm very sorry; but I will ask my sister to make some to-morrow," innocently replied our little heroine.

"Humph! do you suppose I'm going to stand here till to-morrow waiting for them?" said the crusty old lady, as she turned away and was lost in the crowd. Next came a jolly-looking old gentleman, with a broad, ruddy face, and a pair of twinkling eyes, that would not stay still long enough for you to tell what color they were. He paused directly before Eva, and, leaning with both hands on his gold-headed cane, he surveyed her and her wares for a moment in silence. Then, in a rich, cheery voice, that rang out through his white mustache like the sound of sleigh bells through a fall of snow, he exclaimed, "Well, little girl, you have some mighty pretty things here; I wonder if there is not something that will do for my little boy." At the last word Eva's countenance fell, and she looked dubiously at her collection of toys; then turning her eyes pleadingly to the great, good-natured face that was looking down upon her, she said earnestly, "I don't believe that I have a single thing that a boy would like; but have you not a little girl, who would want a bonnet or a chair for her doll ? "

The fleshy gentleman indulged in a short, merry laugh ; then suddenly looking very grave, he said, " Why, no ! I can't say that I have any little girl of my own, but then, you know, if one should come to see me, it would be very nice to have the playthings all ready ; so I will take a bonnet, and a chair too, but you must select them, for I can't tell which is the prettiest. And what is this ? " he continued, while Eva was conscientiously endeavoring to decide as to the respective merits of a red chair and a green one.

" That, sir," she answered, hastily concluding in favor of the red, and looking up to see what it was he held in his hand, " that is a workbasket."

" A workbasket, is it ? " said the odd old gentleman, with a chuckle that made his broad sides shake again ; " well, I should think that would hold just such a homœopathic dose of work as my wife will be likely to accomplish, so I will take that too. Now, what is my bill ? " he added, taking out his purse with a flourish. Eva slowly counted upon her fingers the value of his purchases, and then, in a voice that trembled with fear lest he should be angry at the magnitude of the sum, announced it to be seventy-five cents.

" Well, there—never mind the change, child ; " and away went the great fat man, with the gay little basket dangling at his finger ends, while in Eva's lap lay a bright gold dollar, looking all the brighter from contrast with her black dress.

The child began to think she was in a fair way to make her fortune, and could not help indulging in one or two joyful little hops, when she thought how glad Lilian would be to hear of her good luck. But just then two great boys came loitering along, with what seemed a number of strings hanging over their shoulders.

" Come, let's stop here, Bill," said one to his companion, as he stepped directly in front of Eva, and blew a shrill blast on a brass whistle which he held in his hand. The little girl was not much pleased with her new neighbors, particularly when she discovered that at the end of each of the strings that they carried was suspended a large artificial spider, which, with long, quivering legs and bloated bodies, bore so close a resemblance to the ugly reptile which they were intended to imitate, that she felt almost afraid of them, although she well knew they were only bits of wood and wire. She kept very quiet, earnestly hoping that the boys would move on; but they showed no disposition to do so. The shrill noise of the whistle was kept up incessantly, and they jerked their ugly toys about, making them squirm and wriggle in a most hideous manner, much to Eva's disgust, though greatly to the delight of a crowd of boys who had collected around them, and were vociferously striving to make them lower the price of the spiders to correspond with the state of their own finances. As yet they had taken no notice of Eva, and she began to think how she could escape from their vicinity without attracting their attention, when one of them, stepping backward, threw himself against the fence, never heeding that, as he did so, the long, ragged skirt of his coat swept her basket to the ground, and quite spoiled the tasteful arrangement of her entire stock.

"Hello, Tom!" exclaimed his comrade, "you're knocking that young un's things all into pi; why can't you move on?"

"What do I care for the young un, or her things either?" gruffly returned Tom, at the same time swinging one of his horrid spiders in the face of Eva, who had stooped to rescue her property, which lay so dangerously near his feet. The poor child could not suppress a cry of terror, at which the boys raised a malicious laugh, even Bill joining in their mirth, as if ashamed that he had shown himself less brutal than the others. Eva hastily repacked her basket, and, escaping from the noisy throng, made her way back to the good black woman's side.

" Please let me sit near you," she pleaded, laying her little trembling hand on the brawny arm of her friend ; " I am afraid of those boys."

" What's dem been a doin' to yer ? Only let me git a hold of 'em, an' I'll——" ' What she would have done, in case they had fallen into her hands, could only be inferred from the energetic manner in which she shook her fist toward them ; for, as she started up to carry her vague threat into effect, Eva caught her hand, exclaiming, " Don't do anything to them ; indeed they did not hurt me—they only frightened me, and that, you know," she continued, as her champion resumed her seat, " that, you know, they cannot do again if you let me stay by you."

" Let yer stay by me, chile ? ob course I will, and be mighty glad ob yer company, too. And even if I wa'n't, why, honey, dis is a free country, and eberybody has a right to go or stay whar dey's a mind to,"

Eva opened her eyes very wide at this new declaration of independence, but her honest friend, without heeding her astonishment, talked on, while she once more helped her to arrange her temporary counter.

" Now, chile, it'll be rale nice to have yer so nigh; it'll be somebody to speak to onc't in a while. I'd a had yer here at fust, only I tought maybe if yer was off by yerself the folks would feel more kinder sorry like for yer, and more likely buy yer things; but lor', honey, it's jest the same as if yer was alone now, for a blind man could see dat sech a little picter as you be, wid yer white face and yeller hair, couldn't belong to Nancy Jenkins."

" What is it you say about the blind man, Mrs. Jenkins? You mistake; the blind man no can tell the fair face from the dark, but he know the beauty of good deeds and kind words; so if the little child have a good heart, and speak the good words, then the blind man say she have beauty like Mrs. Jenkins—perhaps she her little child."

Eva looked up at the speaker with a half amused, half pitying expression on her bright little face. It was the old organ grinder, who, wearied with his fruitless labor, had drawn closer to Mrs. Jenkins' fruit stand,

6

and, while he stood resting his instrument against the fence, overheard the conversation between the good woman and her little protégée. Mrs. Jenkins (for so we must hereafter call Eva's humble friend) turned toward him with a laugh, exclaiming, " Lor', Mr. Anthony! you"—but just then a customer presented himself, and she left her sentence unfinished: as the old man presently resumed his grinding, there was no occasion to renew the subject; so Eva, as well as you and I, was left in the dark as to what reply Mrs. Jenkins would have made to the foreigner's compliment.

Eva watched the old man with much interest. How quickly the pleasant smile, that had lighted up his face while he spoke, faded away, and the mournful expression that seemed habitual returned. She quite forgot her own troubles in sympathy for the unknown sorrow of the aged stranger; and when, from time to time, a compassionate passer-by dropped a penny into his outstretched hand, she felt as glad as if some good fortune had befallen herself. But you must not think our little heroine had nothing to do but watch her neighbors. She must keep an eye on her goods, to see that no evil happened to them, and answer the number-

less questions as to the price of this or that,
which were asked and answered so often to
no purpose; and when she did occasionally
effect a sale, what a tax it was on her arith-
metic to make the change!   She was very
busy, I assure you, all that cold winter's day,
and, when the early twilight began to gather
its shadows over the city, she was very glad
to pack up the remaining toys and hurry
home.   But first she paused to bid Mrs. Jenkins good-bye, and tell her that she would be
there again in the morning.   Then stepping
quickly up to the blind man, and slipping a
half dime into his hand, she bounded away;
nor was it long before she was seated on her
sister's lap, telling the adventures of the day.
Lilian was both surprised and rejoiced at the
success of her little sister's experiment.   She
had passed a sad, lonely day, striving in vain
to think of some way by which she might
procure bread for herself and the child whom
her dying mother had committed to her care.
Her cough had been more than usually
troublesome, and she would start with terror,
and strive to shake off the feeling of lassitude,
as she thought, "What will become of Eva if
I die?"   She longed for the child's return,
though she doubted not it would be empty-
handed, as she went; and, as hour after hour

passed by without her coming, she grew fearful lest some accident had befallen her.   But
now this greatest trouble was at an end; she
held the little wanderer safe in her arms, and
could hardly believe her senses as she counted
out, from the purse that she had placed empty
in her hands that morning, two whole dollars.
Oh! how Eva enjoyed her surprise, and what
a nice supper they had that night, and what
a famous appetite the little merchant brought
to bear upon it, and how sweetly she slept,
when she had said her prayers and thanked
the good God for taking care of her through
all that eventful day.

CHAPTER XII.

FOR many succeeding days Eva might have been seen regularly at her post. In spite of the hard times, people were looking forward to the holidays, and this made trade brisk for our young merchant. Indeed, Lilian, with her aching head and racking cough, found it difficult to make the supply meet the demand. Ah! there was the one drawback to Eva's happiness. She did not mind that the cold pinched her fingers and benumbed her feet, while sitting or standing all day long in the open air; she cared not that she had no time to play, and but an hour or two in the early morning for study—all this was merely her own loss or inconvenience; and if ever she felt like repining, she had only to look at "little Faith" treading her stony, wave-washed path, and her cheerful courage would return. But when she saw her sweet sister Lillie daily growing paler and more languid, and listened to her hollow cough as she plied her ever busy needle, her little heart would swell, and the tears would fill her bright eyes, in spite of her efforts to keep them down. Still she was on the whole a happy little thing. Mrs. Jenkins continued to be her fast friend, the old organ man's mournful face would light up with a smile of welcome when he heard her voice, and if she left home feeling ever so sadly in the morning, hope kept whispering to her all the way, "Lillie will be better to-morrow," until she felt quite sure it must be so, and ten chances to one she would join her humble friends with a song on her lips, and all the tears in her eyes turned to bright sparkles.

One morning, however, she came later than usual, and Mrs. Jenkins, who was watching for her with some anxiety, was alarmed as she saw with what slow, languid steps she approached, and that her sweet face wore a look of distress, such as she had never seen there before.

" Why, what's der matter wid yer, honey ! " she exclaimed, opening her arms to receive her little favorite. Eva, unable to speak, hid her face on the good woman's bosom and sobbed aloud.

"Lor' sakes! don't cry so, chile, but jes' tell old Aunty what troubles her pet."

Thus urged, Eva checked her sobs, and in a few broken words told the cause of her grief. Lilian was sick, so sick as to be unable to rise from her bed, and the undefined fear with which the child had looked at her flushed face and marked her labored breathing, was increased to absolute terror when she overheard Mrs. Havens say to one of her boarders, "I don't believe that poor girl will ever live through this attack. Hard work and trouble have about used up what little strength she had to begin with."

Poor little Eva! the cloud which had thus suddenly gathered about her was so very dark that even the eye of faith with which she had learned to look beyond her many trials was at first unable to pierce its obscurity. She would gladly have remained with her sister, but it was more than ever necessary that she should earn something to supply their increasing wants; so when Jennie Havens came to the room and said that her mother had sent her to sit with Lilian, she took up her basket, and for the first time went reluctantly to her self-appointed task. But, as we have seen, there were those awaiting her who were ready to share her grief, and to impart all the

consolation it was in their power to give.
Indeed, good, honest-hearted Mrs. Jenkins
told of so many people who had been "tuck
in jest sech a way," who were " well and
hearty now," that the child felt somewhat
comforted, and the blind man's words of sympathy, mingled as they were with the musical
terms of endearment that enrich his own lan-
guage, were very soothing to her little aching
heart.   Still the day passed wearily, and she
longed for its close, that she might hasten
back to Lilian's bedside.

It was almost with joy that she hailed
the first glimmering of the street lights, the
signal which released her from her post.   She
was hurrying her remaining toys into the basket, when Mrs. Jenkins laid her hand on her
shoulder, saying, " Look-a-here, honey, yer
jes' tell me der number ob yer house, an' den
jes' as soon as I've seed Mr. Anthony home
(yer know I allus do that since his little gran'-
son's been sick), an' stopped in ter see how
my ole man's gettin' along, I'll come round
ter fin' out how yer sister is, an' maybe I can
be of some kind er sarvice."

This was the very thing that Eva had
been wishing for all day ; but she knew how
little leisure time her friend had, and did not
quite like to ask her to take so long a walk

after the day's toil. Now, however, that she had herself made the proposition, the child was not slow to express her pleasure at the proposed visit, and repeating for the third or fourth time, "Number eighty-two; please don't forget to come, Mrs. Jenkins," she caught up her basket and hastened away. She still bore a heavy heart, but already there were gleams of brightness breaking through the clouds that shut out her sunlight, and she began once more to hope "Lillie would be better to-morrow," and to look with her old faith to the guiding hand of her Heavenly Father.

She had need of all the comfort that hope and faith could bring to her when she reached home, and, creeping noiselessly to her sister's bedside, saw the change that a few hours had wrought. Lilian's eyes were wandering wildly from object to object, while she talked constantly of the scenes familiar to her childhood, as if she thought she was still a child in her dear old home. Poor little Eva, frightened at her strange manner, caught her hand, crying out, "Don't look so, Lillie! oh, speak to me!" but the restless eyes, after turning upon her for a moment with a vacant gaze, wandered away again without a sign of recognition.

Mrs. Havens, who was sitting by the bed, rose, and, taking the terrified child by the hand, led her to the opposite side of the room.

" Eva," she said in a low voice, " your sister is very sick indeed. She has been out of her head for more than two hours. You must not try to talk to her, for she does not know you, and it will only worry her."

" Won't she ever know me again ? " sobbed Eva, the tears rolling down her little pale face.

" Hush ! Yes, I hope so ; but you must be quiet now, and listen to me ; " then, after waiting a moment for the little girl to conquer her emotion, she continued : " I have sent Jennie for a doctor—he has not come yet ; but I am afraid this is a very dangerous illness, and that your sister will be sick a long time, even if she recovers at last. Have you no friends who could take her to their home, or at least come here and take care of her ? " Eva shook her head, and her tears burst forth afresh. " Then, child," she resumed in a troubled voice, " I am afraid she must go where she can receive better attendance than I am able to give. At the hospital she would be well cared for, without any expense, and I think, Eva, that, if the doctor says she can be moved without danger, it will be best to send her there."

Mrs. Havens had endeavored to break the subject cautiously and kindly to the little orphan, and was not prepared for the passionate burst of grief and dismay with which it was received.

" You sha'n't send my sister away to that horrid place ! " she exclaimed, crying as if her very heart would break. All efforts that Mrs. Havens made to soothe her were for a time useless, for Eva shrank from her as if she considered her a heartless enemy. Finally, raising the little quivering form to her lap, she said sadly, " My child, I am very sorry for you and for Lilian ; you must not think what I have been saying was spoken in unkindness. I should be very glad to keep her here, but it is impossible. How could we even pay the physician's fee? I am poor myself, Eva."

" Oh ! " exclaimed the child, brightening, " I can make money enough for that ; see, I made all this to-day," and she emptied the contents of her purse upon the table.

" I see you have done very well ; but you must remember that Lilian will not be able to make any more articles for you to sell. Then there is still another objection to your sister's remaining here. She will require constant watching and attention; you are too young to be trusted, and I don't see what time I can have for it. You know that, since Ellen went out West and I dismissed Bridget, I have all the house work to do, and no one to help me in anything."

Eva saw the truth of all this, and.sat for a moment lost in thought; then, looking up, she said : "I am sorry I spoke so naughty to you, Mrs. Havens. You know better than I what ought to be done ; but mayn't I go with Lillie ? "

"We will talk about that some other time. Here comes the doctor ;" and Mrs. Havens, hastily kissing the child, put her from her lap, and, stepping to the door, admitted the physician, whose footstep she had heard on the stairs.

Dr. H—— pronounced Lilian's illness to be of a very serious character, and agreed with Mrs. Havens that, under the circumstances, it would be best to take her to the hospital. He promised to make all necessary arrangements, and to come himself in the morning to superintend the removal.

"Please let me go with my sister," pleaded little Eva, laying her dimpled hand on his, as he turned the door-knob to leave the room ; "please let me go with my sister."

"Why, that is impossible, my poor child,"

he said pityingly; "but don't cry, you shall be taken care of." Then turning to Mrs. Havens: "You say, ma'am, that they are orphans and without friends; would it not be well to get the little one admitted into one of the orphan asylums?"

"Oh, dear, no!" replied the good lady, in evident distress. "It is bad enough to send Lilian away when it is for her own good. The child can just as well stay here as not; she will be no kind of trouble to me; she is such a smart little thing, she can take care of herself."

"There, my dear," said the doctor, stroking Eva's curls, "you must be a good girl, and not cry any more. Mrs. Havens is very kind to keep you here. I hope your sister will soon be better, and I will see that you are allowed to visit her every day while she is at the hospital."

This promise was some consolation to the poor child, and, feeling that she must prove herself worthy of the privilege, she dried her eyes and determinately kept down the sobs that were struggling for utterance. When Dr. H—— had gone, Mrs. Havens stationed her at Lilian's bedside, telling her to remain there and keep very still, while she "ran down to see about the tea." Eva had been

sitting some time in the darkened room, listening in silent dread to her sister's unconscious mutterings, and striving not to think
of to-morrow, when, hearing a gentle tap at
the door, she softly opened it, and there, to
her unspeakable joy, stood her friend the
apple woman, whose kind, dark face seemed
really beautiful to the weary, sorrowful child.

As soon as she understood the exact state
of the case, Mrs. Jenkins announced her de-
termination to stay all night and make herself generally useful, much to the relief of
Mrs. Havens and the satisfaction of Eva, who
felt the cheering influence of her pleasant
voice, and quiet though bustling industry, as
she busied herself about the rooms, " putting
things to rights," as she called it.

At last Lilian, quieted by the effect of
medicine that Dr. H—— had left for her, fell
asleep. This, Mrs. Jenkins whispered to Eva,
was a " berry favo'ble sign," and, leading her
into the other room the good woman made
her sit in her little chair by the fire, while she
toasted a slice of bread and warmed a cup of
milk for her. When the dainty repast was
ready, she took the little girl on her lap, and,
by means of coaxing, succeeded in making
her eat it. As soon as this was accomplished,
she pushed aside the dishes, settled herself

back in her chair, and, drawing Eva's head to her bosom, she said, " Now, little missey, ole Nancy'll tell yer a' story. What shall it be about, honey ? "

" Oh, about yourself. I like true stories," said Eva, glad that good Mrs. Jenkins' endless talking left her so little time to think of the dreaded parting with her sister.

" Well, now, jes' ter hear de chile ! How d'ye know that thar is any story ter tell about me ? I s'pose, though, a'most eberybody's had some kind of sperance that, if it was writ out all proper like, would make a pretty good story ; so if yer raly wants ter know how I'se got along so far through de worl', why, I'll jes' tell yer. Yer see, honey, I was raised down in Virginny, on a big plantation, where thar was lots of colored pussons, big an' little, ole an' young. A mighty nice time I had ob it when I was a chile, a-playin' about wid de oder chil'en. Much *we* car'd weder we was white or black, so long as we had plenty to eat an' nuthin' ter do but play from mornin' ter night ! But at last I grew ter be a great, tall gal, an' Missis had me up ter de house tu learn tu sew an' fit work, kase she meant I should be a seamstress, an' work in de house, instead of habin' ter go out ter de fields like some ob de gals had ter. Yer see she had

tuk a shine ter me, and wanted ter do me all
de good she could. Now, honey, I really believe my missis was a perfect angel, even
when she libed in dis miser'ble worl', an' I
knows for sartin she is now, for she went
home ter de better country a long time ago;
but massa was quite a different sort ob a pus-
son. He thought all de worl' ob missis, an'
dat was de only good p'int dar was about
him. Lor'! how he would storm an' swar
an' lash his whip about when t'ings didn't
suit him. Howsomever, he didn't hab 'casion
ter storm at *me* much, for my work was all
for missis, an' it didn't consarn him nuthin'
how it was done. Well, it was a dark day
for all ob us when de missis took sick an' de
doctor said she wouldn't neber goin' fur to be
any better. Trouble had a bery curious 'fect
on massa. He was more onreasonable an'
'zacting than eber, an' we was 'most afraid ob
our libes. Now yer see, honey, I had been
married ter Cato den about two years. Cato
was one ob de field han's, an' a right smart
fellow he was in dem days, though he's got
de rhumatis powerful bad now. One day,
when missis was at de worse, I was a-sittin'
at our little cabin door a-gettin' my baby ter
sleep, an' a-thinkin' how sad it would be
when our good, kind missis should be took

away from us, when all ter onc't Cato rushed
in wid his eyes a-starin' an' his teeth a chat-
terin', an' a-lookin' so drefful dat it skeered
me a'most ter death. Jes' as soon as he could
speak, he cried out, 'Oh, Nancy, Nancy,
massa is gwine ter sell you an' de baby to-
morrow, to be carried clean off down South!'
An' den he trowed hisself on de floor, an'
clutched his har wid both hands, an' groaned
awful. I got right up. 'Cato,' says I, 'take
keer ob de chile;' so he sat up on de floor
an' looked at me questionin' like; but I jes'
put little Tommy into his arms, an' walked
straight tu de house, an' right into missis'
room. Massa was thar, but I didn't keer for
him den; I pushed past him when he tried
ter stop me, an', gwine right ter missis' bedside, I told her jes' how it was. Den, weak
as she was, she started up in bed, and looked
massa in de face. 'John,' says she, 'will you
do dis thing?' He kep' a-pokin' at his boot
wid a little switch he held in his hand, an'
mumbled somet'ing about 'raisin' money;'
but missis wouldn't listen to him. She began
a-talkin' to him so beautiful an' solemn like,
and neber gave up till he promised to set
Cato an' me free, an' den she wouldn't be
satisfied till he sent off for a lawyer an' had
free papers made out for us an' for little Tom-

my too ; kase, yer see, I reckon she knowed that massa wouldn't be likely ter keep a promis', even ter her, if it took de money outer his pocket, so she meant ter make suro of it wid de lawyer 'fore she died. An' mighty thankful Cato an' I were ter her for thinkin' so much about us, an' she a-dyin'! I tell yer, honey, eider ob us would have been glad ter gib our life ter save her's after dat. But it couldn't be, an' it wan't many days 'fore de good Lord sent an' took her ter de hebbenly home."

Here the old woman paused to wipe a tear from her eye with the corner of her checked apron. That tear, in memory of one who was her friend in the dark days of her bondage, was a richer tribute than the costliest monument ever raised to one whom fame or station had rendered great. It would shine with purer lustre than a diamond, in the crown of blessedness that would circle the brow of the " good missis " in that day when the Judge of all the world shall say, "Inasmuch as ye have done it unto one of the least of these, ye have done it unto me."

After a moment's silence Mrs. Jenkins went on with her story: "Ah! chile, dat were a heavy day to all ob us poor niggers. Even Cato an' I didn't seem to feel much comfort in thinkin' we was free, kase it were so drefful ter think ob gwine off an' leavin' so many ob our friends ter de mercy ob such a cruel massa; for, after missis died, he seemed ter go kinder crazy, an 'peared like he were 'sessed ob an ebel spirit. I r'ally do think dat de little good dare eber was in him was buried in her grave. But dare wan't no good in our stayin', eben if we could, so Cato an' I, we bundled up what little things we had, an' made our way to de free States de bes' way we could. An' here we's been in dis yer big city more'n thirty years. Sometimes we's got along fus'-rate, an' sometimes we's been pretty bad off; but somehow de Lord He's allus took keer ob us, an' den we an' our chil'en is *free*, an' dat is a great comfort.

"Tommy, he's married, an' is doin' fus'-rate in de white-washin' business. My darter aint very strong; she lives at home wid Cato an' me, an' she takes keer ob her father while I'm out; den, too, she 'casionally helps us 'siderably a-doin' odd jobs for de neighbors. So we manage ter get along; an' yer know, honey, we's only told ter ax, 'Give us *dis day* our daily bread.' "

Long before Mrs. Jenkins finished her story, Eva's eyelids had been drooping drowsily, but, the last words partly arousing her,

she folded her little hands, and silently repeated the prayer of which they are part.
Then sleepily opening her eyes for a moment,
they fell upon the beautiful statuette of Faith,
which the black woman had taken in her
hand, and was looking at with wonder and
admiration.

As soon as Mrs. Jenkins was sure that her
little charge was asleep, she gently undressed
her and laid her on the lounge; then seated
herself by Lilian's bedside to watch her fitful
slumbers. Sometimes she nodded in her
chair, it is true, but she never failed to ad-
minister the medicine at exactly the right
time.

Eva awoke the next morning with a sense
of some impending evil, though it was several
moments before she could collect her scattered thoughts sufficiently to remember exactly what misfortune she dreaded; but when
full recollection came to her, she started up
in terror, lest they should have taken her
sister away already. Stealing softly to the
open door of Lilian's room, she was relieved
to find she was still there, and Mrs. Jenkins
at her bedside. The latter beckoned her to
come in, and to her eager question, " How is
sister Lillie now ? " replied in a whisper,
" She ha'n't took no notice of nuthin' dis

mornin', but we ought to be thankful ter see her lyin' so quiet an' peaceful, 'stead ob ravin' like she was yesterday."

Eva turned away without speaking, and commenced dressing as hastily as her little trembling hands would permit.

After a while Mrs. Havens came up. Mrs. Jenkins was then making a cup of coffee for their breakfast, and Eva had taken her place by the bedside. The little girl could hear her two friends consulting together in low tones, and felt an uneasy consciousness that she was the subject of their conversation. And so in fact she was. Mrs. Havens knew that she did not intend to go out with her basket as usual this morning. She dreaded to have her present when Lilian was moved, yet did not like to tell her that she should not stay; so she appealed to the old fruit woman to persuade the child to accompany her when she went to her stand.

Mrs. Jenkins agreed that it would be a great trial to the little girl to see her sister carried helpless and unconscious from the place which had been so long their home, and promised to coax her to go. Accordingly, as soon as she had washed up the breakfast dishes, she said in a cheerful tone:

"Now, honey, get yer basket an' come 'long wid ole Nancy."

"Oh, no, no!" please don't ask me to go to-day, Mrs. Jenkins," said Eva in reply, shrinking nearer to the door of Lilian's room.

"Jes' come yere a minit, my little pet," said Mrs. Jenkins, drawing the reluctant child to her knee. "Now don't yer go ter cry; dare aint nobody gwine ter make yer go nowhar dat yer dont want'er, but yer jes' hear what I've got ter say, an' I reckon yer'll 'clude ter go yerself. Thar's Miss Lillie, now, she don't eben know yer dis mornin', an' it won't make a mite ob difference wid her wedder yer's here or whar yer be. Dar aint nothin' yer kin do for her but what de doctor an' de nuss at de hospital kin do a great sight better. So wouldn't yer ruther go now, when she don't need yer, an' 'arn some money, so that when she gets better in a few days yer kin buy some nice things for her? An' look a-yere, honey, if yer'll go wid me now, jes' as soon as de doctor says she kin eat it, I'll gib yer de biggest orange I kin find for her."

Eva sat still, with the tears rolling slowly over her cheeks, but, evidently impressed by Mrs. Jenkins' argument; presently she looked up, and said in a low voice, "I will go; but let me kiss Lillie first."

"Dat yer may, honey!" exclaimed the

good woman, hastily dashing her rough hand across her eyes.

In a few moments more, Eva and her dusky friend were walking rapidly toward the place of their humble avocation. They found the blind organ grinder already at his post, Mrs. Jenkins' daughter having led him there, as had been agreed she should do the evening before.

Eva's stock of goods was small now, and, though she sold but little during the day, she had only two or three articles left when evening came.

" Now, look-a-yere, chile," said Mrs. Jenkins, when it was time to *shut up shop*, " yer jes' come 'long wid me while I totes dese yere t'ings home, an' gets Mr. Anthony safe ter his house, den I'se gwine ter take yer ter see yer sister."

The little girl's face brightened; she had supposed that she must wait until the next day before being admitted to the hospital, and had been slowly preparing to return home, feeling how desolate that lonely home would be. But the hope of seeing Lilian gave her new life; she started up eagerly, and stood watching Mrs. Jenkins' deliberate movements, until, unable to check her impatience longer, she ventured to ask, " Won't we be too late if we don't hurry ? "

"I reckon not, chile, but den p'r'aps it's jes' as well not ter be too slow;" and she packed away her fruit with rather less delay.

How rejoiced Eva was when she saw the last rosy-cheeked apple disappear within the capacious basket, the cover close over it, and the basket itself, with all its luscious burden, swung securely on one of the stout arms of its owner, while the other offered a strong support to the blind man! Then the trio set forth. They were all unheeded by the hurrying crowds through which they moved, and yet there was a pathos in their very companionship more touching, a heroism in each of their humble lives more noble than that which, when depicted on the page of romance, had many a time awakened the sensibility or stirred the admiration of those who passed them by so carelessly.

After passing through several streets, such as Eva had never seen before, dark, dirty, and ill smelling, thronging with wretched men and women, and still more wretched children, they turned down a narrow alley, which, though more quiet, was hardly less miserable, where, stopping before a dilapidated old building, the blind man released Mrs. Jenkins' arm, and, bidding God bless her for her kindness to him, he slowly de-

scended the flight of rickety steps that led to
the basement, or rather cellar, of the forlorn
edifice. Mrs. Jenkins took Eva's hand, and
walked rapidly on a few paces in silence;
then, as if struck with a sudden thought, she
turned back, and, still leading the wondering
child, followed the old organ grinder into his
subterranean home. Never had Eva's bright
eyes opened upon such a scene of misery as
they now beheld, as soon as they became
enough accustomed to the darkness to distin-
guish the objects by which she was surrounded. The old man had unstrapped the organ
from his weary shoulders and placed it carefully in one corner of the room, and was now
seated on an inverted tub, striving to warm
his half-frozen fingers over a handful of coals
that were smouldering in an earthen furn
on the hearth. A tallow candle, stuck into a
broken bottle, and standing on an old barrel
in place of a table, cast its feeble light over
the pale face of a sickly looking woman, who,
kneeling on the damp floor at his side, was
eagerly counting the few pennies that he had
gathered during thé day.

The woman started up when she saw Mrs.
Jenkins, and, seizing her hand, drew her toward something at the side of the room which
had escaped Eva's notice in her first hasty

7

glance over the dreary abode. This something, which in the general darkness seemed at first only a darker shadow, proved upon closer examination to be a bundle of straw covered with rags, upon which lay the form of a little boy about her own age. Around him was wrapped a blanket shawl, which, though faded and somewhat worn, was by far the most comfortable article that the poor family seemed to possess. The sleeping child clutched it with his little bony fingers, as if he feared it would be taken from him. The woman, still holding Mrs. Jenkins' hand, stooped and stroked the shawl in a caressing manner, as if it were a living thing; then raising herself and pointing down to the boy, she exclaimed, " See! Luigi sleep now—shawl warm, warm! 'Ou good, 'ou like angel—me t'ank!" She could say no more, for the excitement, together with the effort she had made to master the few words of English, brought on a violent paroxysm of coughing, and Eva was horrified to see that, when it had passed, the apron she held to her lips was stained with blood.

'Mrs. Jenkins stepped to the table, or rather *barrel*, and, unobserved by those for whom the little charity was intended, placed a dime among the pennies which the poor woman had left lying there. As she did so, Eva perceived for the first time that the shawl she had on was much smaller than the one she usually wore, and, glancing again at the humble bed by which she was still standing, the little girl discovered that the covering, which was so gratefully prized, was the very one that had so long shielded the old fruit woman's form from the keen winter blasts. She had but just made this discovery, when Mrs. Jenkins took her hand and led her up into the street again.

It was not so dark outdoors as in the organ grinder's burrow-like home; still, the dusk was deepening, and they walked rapidly onward. Nothing was said for several moments; then, as a bitter cold blast swept past them, Eva looked up and said:

" Did you give away your nice warm shawl, Mrs. Jenkins ? "

" Lor', chile! dat's nuthin'; dis yere is good enough for me. Anyhow, I kin stan' der cole better'n yonder sick baby, I reckon."

While talking they had turned into a more open street; the buildings were all of a very humble description, but there was an air of cleanliness and hopefulness, quite in contrast with the dirty alley they had just left.

" Here's whar I live, honey," said Mrs.

Jenkins, as they entered the outer door of a decent looking tenement house. She led Eva up two or three flights of stairs; then, opening a door at the end of the hall, ushered her into her own neat, cheerful home.

By the fire sat old Cato, propped up in his rocking chair. Sally, his daughter, was busy with preparations for supper, and a large gray cat, that lay on a bit of carpet before the fire, was purring a drowsy accompaniment to the tea-kettle's song.

" Why! mother, you are home early to-night," said Sally, hastening to take the basket from her hand; " and you have brought the little girl—that's nice ! "

" Hoity, toity ! " cried Cato, who had just caught sight of little Eva, " whar yer come from, little pinky posey ? Come an' see ole Cato, an' tell um all 'bout it."

The child went to him, and, while she was trying to answer his questions, and thinking how odd he looked with his white hair and black face, Mrs. Jenkins held a whispered conversation with her daughter, in which she told her all that had taken place with regard to the orphans, and of her promise to go with Eva to the hospital this evening. " So now, Sally," she continued, in a louder tone, " I'll jes' take a cup ob dis yere hot tea, an' be off; don't keep yer supper a-waitin' for me, but jes' sot a plate ob sumthin' down ter der fire ter keep warm till I get back." While she was speaking, Sally had taken a nice raised biscuit from the oven, and buttered it for Eva. It was very acceptable to the poor child, for grief and anxiety had robbed her of appetite during the day, and she began to feel quite hungry after her long walk.

"Now, honey, I reckon we'd better go," said Mrs. Jenkins, as soon as Eva had finished her biscuit. She eagerly obeyed the summons, and in a moment more they were again threading their way through the crowded streets.

They soon reached the hospital, but what was little Eva's disappointment when told that they could not be admitted, no visitors being allowed at that hour! In vain were her tears and Mrs. Jenkins' expostulations; such was the rule, and it could not be set aside. Mrs. Jenkins was about giving it up, when, glancing at the sorrowful face of the child, she determined to make one more effort in her behalf. She had just commenced her remonstrance anew, and the porter had begun to show signs of impatience, when a gentleman, passing through the hall, came forward to learn the cause of the dispute. Eva, recognizing him as the physician who had attended Lilian, sprang toward him, exclaiming :

"You said I might see my sister every day, and now that man won't let me."

"Not so fast, my little girl, not so fast!" said Dr. II——, smiling ; "I said you might see her every *day*, not every *night*. There is a difference, which you and your good friend here seem to have overlooked."

Eva stood still a moment with drooping, tearful eyes ; then looking up, she said softly :

"I am sorry I didn't understand you ; but if I can't see Lillie to-night, may I come to-morrow ? and will you please tell me how she is now ? "

"She is, I think, somewhat better than in the morning ; she is sleeping quietly. But come, little one, you shall not be disappointed. It was very careless on my part not to tell you at what time you could be admitted ; so now I will take you myself to see your sister, if you will promise to be very quiet and not disturb her."

Dr. H—— led Eva, followed by Mrs. Jenkins, up stairs and into a long, dimly lighted room. On each side of the room stood a number of cot beds at equal distances from each other. Eva observed, as she passed, that some were occupied and others not, but that all looked neat and comfortable. On one of these cots, at the farther end of the apartment, Lilian was lying in a gentle slumber. By her side was seated a pleasant looking woman, engaged in knitting. She whispered a few kind words to the child, as she made way for her to come near the bed. The sweet voice in which they were spoken, rather than the words themselves, won the confidence of her little heart, and she felt almost reconciled to leaving Lilian in this strange place, if she was to have so gentle a nurse. Indeed, while the little girl stood beside her sleeping sister, much of the dread she had felt when thinking of her as an inmate of the hospital disappeared. To be sure, it was not the pleasantest place in the world—not even so pleasant as their own humble home; but, as she looked at the tidy bed, and glanced around the warm yet airy room, she thought of the organ grinder's cellar, and of the sick boy wrapped in Mrs. Jenkins' shawl, and she resolved not only to repine no longer at her own lot, but to try and do something to aid those who were still more unfortunate.

Presently Dr. H—— took her hand to lead her away; she longed to give her sister

one kiss, but he shook his head, and drew her
gently from the bedside. When they were
going down the stairs, he told her that, if
Lilian could sleep undisturbed for a few
hours, she would probably awake with restored consciousness. "And so, my little
girl," he said, cheerfully, "when you come
to-morrow morning, you may give her as
many kisses as you please, though it would
not do this evening."

When Eva reached home her heart was
much lighter than when she went out in the
morning. She no longer feared that her
sister would die, for had not the doctor
assured her that she would be better to-morrow? And then, after all, the hospital was
not such a dreadful place as she had supposed; so she said "Good-by" to Mrs. Jenkins, and thanked her for the trouble she had
taken for her in quite a cheerful voice.

It was very lonely for the little orphan as
she sat by the fire, eating her bread and
milk; but she tried to drive all sad thoughts
away, and for company's sake seated her doll
in a chair by her side, and played that she
shared her supper. Then she washed the
bowl and spoon, and put them away, and,
taking her little Testament, she read over her
Sunday school lesson; then closing the book,

she sat watching the red and blue flames that kept dancing up to peep at her through the open door of the stove, until somehow they were all at once changed into familiar forms and faces. There were Mrs. Jenkins and the blind man, old Cato and Dr. H——, Lilian and Sally and Mrs. Havens, all dancing a most fantastic jig; but just as old Cato cut a double pigeon wing, and tossed his crutch in the air, she was aroused by a sudden crash, and started up to find that she had been almost asleep and quite dreaming, and that her doll had fallen out of her arms upon the hearth. She picked it up and anxiously examined it; to her no small comfort she found there was no damage done, but concluded that it was high time both she and Dolly were in bed.

"You shall sleep with me to-night, Dolly!" she said, as she took off its pink silk dress, and put on the nice little nightgown that Lilian had made for it. Though Eva tried so hard to be cheerful, she could not help feeling very disconsolate as for the first time she prepared to go to bed alone. She strove not to think of her loneliness, but of the pleasant times she should have when Lilian was well and at home again. Still the tears would rush from her full heart to her eyes, till they

7*

almost blinded her ; but she quickly brushed them away, and, kneeling by the bedside, uttered her simple prayer to the Father of the fatherless, and, before many minutes more had passed, was sleeping sweetly with her doll clasped in her arms.

CHAPTER XIII.

It was a very bright ray of sunlight which crept through the drapery that Jack Frost had hung over Eva's bedroom window, and, touching her eyelids, called her back from dreamland. She sprang up at once, and hurried on her clothes, for she remembered that she had a great deal to do that morning. And very busy she was, I assure you. First, there was the fire to make, and a pretty difficult task she found it. How many times it would go quite out, just as she thought it was really beginning to burn! and then she would have the work all to do over again with her little aching fingers. Still she was not discouraged, but labored patiently on, learning a new lesson from every failure, until at last she fairly clapped her hands with delight as the loud roaring and crackling told of her success. Then, while her bread and milk was warming, she made the bed, dusted the room, and dressed her doll. Finally she opened her basket of merchandise, and was somewhat startled as she for the first time realized that her stock in trade was reduced to one needlebook and a pincushion.

" Never mind ! " she said consolingly to herself, " I have some money in my purse yet, and, if I have not much to sell, I need not go out so early, but can wait till it is time to go to see Lillie first."

When she had finished her breakfast, she took her book, thinking to learn a long.lesson before she went, but in vain ; she could not fix her thoughts on what she read. They would constantly wander off, to hover round her sister's sickbed, until at length, giving up the attempt, she threw aside the book and went to the window, where she stood long, watching impatiently the clock in a neighboring church tower till the slowly moving hands pointed to half past nine.

" There ! the doctor said I must be there by ten, so now it is time to go," exclaimed the eager child, as she hurriedly prepared for her cold walk.

Arriving at the hospital, the same woman whose sweet voice had won her confidence the previous evening conducted her up the

long room to Lilian's bedside. The sick girl
had, as Dr. H—— prophesied, awakened
with restored reason. She received Eva with
a smile of pleased recognition.

"Darling little birdie!" she murmured
feebly, smoothing the child's curls. Then,
while a look of pain passed over her face, she
asked, "Who takes care of my little pet
now?"

"Oh, everybody, Lillie!" Eva replied,
with a bright smile; and Lilian was content.
She was too weak as yet to trouble herself
much about her own situation or that of her
sister, so long as the latter seemed well and
happy. Eva saw this, and resolved to appear always as cheerful as possible.

She had been with her sister about an
hour, when Dr. H—— came to make his
daily visit to his patients. Pausing by the
side of Lilian's bed, he seemed pleased,
though not surprised, at the change which
had taken place since the previous evening.
Nodding pleasantly to Eva, and speaking a
few words in a low tone to the nurse, he
passed on to the other patients. Presently
returning, he said kindly to Eva, "You must
come away now, my little girl, and leave
your sister to take a nap. You shall see her
again to-morrow."

When Eva stood on the steps of the hospital with the kind physician, she suddenly looked up into his face and said, somewhat timidly:

"Dr. H——, you have made sister Lillie so much better, that I am sure you could cure a poor little sick boy that I saw last night. Won't you try, please?"

"Why, yes, child," said the doctor, smiling, "I am willing to try my skill on the sick boy, especially as you seem so confident of my success. But who is he, and where does he live?"

"He is the grandson of an old blind organ grinder, and he lives down in a dreadful dark cellar in a narrow, dirty street. But," she continued, with a disturbed look, "I don't know the name of the street, and you could not find it without that, could you?"

"I am afraid not," he replied, trying not to laugh; "I am afraid not, as there are unfortunately quite a number of narrow, dirty streets and dark cellars, with sick boys in them, in this great city."

"Oh, I know now what we can do!" exclaimed Eva, brightening; "Mrs. Jenkins can tell the name of the street. Won't you please come and ask her?"

"Who is Mrs. Jenkins? — your sable friend, though, I suppose; but where must we go to find her?"

"Not very far; she keeps a fruit stand near St. Paul's Church. Won't you come, sir, please?" replied the child, eagerly.

Dr. H—— nodded, took the little girl's hand, and walked with her down Broadway. Mrs. Jenkins gladly gave all the information that was required. The doctor, glancing at his watch, said he had an engagement which would detain him for an hour or two, but promised to call and see little Luigi some time during the day. Then, bidding them a friendly "good-by," he hurried away.

"Now who'd believe de chile would ha' thought ob dat—bress her little heart!" soliloquized Mrs. Jenkins, as she looked proudly at Eva, whom she began to consider as belonging to herself. "It does seem too bad dat she should have ter sit here such wedder as dis," she continued, with a discontent such as she had never felt at her own exposure to the cold; "an' I don't believe she'll sell any more ob dem things either; all de bes' ob 'em is picked out."

But Eva continued patiently at her post, and soon her patience was rewarded. Loitering down the street came a merry-faced boy.

Sticking out of his pockets were divers and sundry packages. He paused to gaze in at all the shop windows as if looking for something, he scarce knew what; as he was passing our little heroine, his eye fell upon her basket.

"That is it!" he exclaimed, looking as if a weight was taken off his mind; then springing to Eva's side, he caught up first the needlebook, then the pincushion, and, glancing into the empty basket, said pleasantly, "Are these all you have left? You must have done a pretty good business this morning to have sold out so soon."

"That is all I had to-day. My sister, who makes the things for me to sell, is sick," she replied gently.

"Oh! that's too bad," exclaimed the boy, casting a pitying look at her, and then a complacent one at the articles in his hand, as he asked, "What is the price of these?"

"The cushion is ten cents, the needlebook fifteen."

"That suits me exactly!" said he, fumbling for his purse, which was at the bottom of his pocket, under all the bundles. "You see," he continued, as the purse came to light, "my uncle gave me a gold dollar not long ago, and I thought I would get all our folks

Christmas presents with it. I got something for everybody but grandma and mother, and I couldn't find anything that I thought would suit them, whose price would suit me, until I came across you. Wasn't it lucky I happened to spy you?" and, handing her a quarter, he ran off with his treasures.

Now that Eva had nothing to sell, there seemed no reason why she should remain any longer out in the cold. Taking up her empty basket, she stepped to Mrs. Jenkins's side to tell her that she was going home; but just then her eye chanced to rest on the poor organ grinder, and a new thought struck her. She could at present do no more to help herself, but might she not do something to aid him? Mrs. Jenkins had told her that, before his little grandson was taken sick, he used to lead him through more retired streets, where he would go from house to house playing his organ, and that then his daily ingathering of small change was much greater than now that he was obliged to stand in the crowded thoroughfare, where the music could not be heard, even if any of the busy throng were disposed to pause and listen.

Why could not she take Luigi's place as the blind man's guide?—Eva asked herself. She could lead him through those beautiful streets where she used to go in the summer to peep at the flowers and listen to the singing birds; and she felt quite certain that the people who lived in such fine houses must be kind and good, and would give something to the poor old blind man. All excitement at the thought of doing good to the sorrowful stranger, Eva confided to Mrs. Jenkins her newly formed plan. The good woman was sorely puzzled as to what she ought to say. She knew that the old man had not received a single penny during the whole morning, and she had no doubt that his chance would be better somewhere else; but then the little child, who seemed in a manner cast under her protection—would she dare let her go wandering off with so helpless a companion? She ventured one or two objections, but Eva was not to be dissuaded, and finally she gave up all attempt to oppose her, saying, "Well, honey, yer must do jes' what yer think yer ought'er, an' de Lord He'll take kere ob both ob yer, I reckon."

Through the broad, quiet streets, where there was fresh, untainted air to breathe and room to walk without jostling one's neighbors, Eva led the blind man. How refreshing was the change! He seemed to draw in new life with every breath of the pure air. How the

music gushed forth from the organ, as if it
meant to make the most of its chance of
being heard ! It leaped away in great waves
of gladness ; it thrilled and warbled, as if a
whole flock of canaries and nightingales were
suddenly let loose ; it poured itself out in a
kind of extravagant wildness, as if it had gone
crazy.with delight ; then changing, it pealed
out in so mournful, so plaintive a strain, that
the tears started to little Eva's eyes in very
sympathy, till, slowly rising and gathering a
sound of sublimity and triumph as it rose, it
seemed to float away beyond the clouds ; and
the child stood looking up to the sky, and
thought of the golden harps around the
Throne.

Many a childish face was pressed against
the window panes of the stately mansions before which the two strangely mated companions paused, and many a penny or half
dime found its way from warm, chubby fingers to the old man's tattered cap.

At one time he was playing some of his
liveliest airs before a house, at the basement
window of which could be seen a pretty little
boy, some two or three years old, seated on
the lap of some one, evidently his nurse.
Presently they lift the window, and in a moment more the little fellow appeared at the

door, 'and, walking up to Eva, said in his baby fashion :

"Mamma has done away, and Betty has not dot any money, but se says I may dive 'ou zese ; " and he held out his apron, which contained several tempting looking cakes.

Eva had eaten nothing since morning, and gladly accepted the offering. The boy watched her remove the cakes from his apron to her own, and, as he shook away the crumbs, said artlessly, " 'Ou is pretty ; Betty says 'ou don't look like ozer ordan ginders' children."

"Willie! Willie! come in now, quick!" called a voice from the house, and Master Willie disappeared in a twinkling.

"I suppose I *don't* look *very* much like a poor child," thought Eva, as she glanced down at her neat, comfortable dress; "but that is because sister Lillie takes such good care of my clothes. Dear sister Lillie! how glad I shall be when she is well again." With a half smothered sigh, she took the blind man's hand and led him to the steps of a church near by, where they sat down to enjoy their unexpected lunch. While thus engaged the old man grew talkative, and finally, in his broken English, told his sad yet simple story to the sympathizing child.

THE ORGAN GRINDER'S STORY.

His name was not Anthony, as good Mrs. Jenkins called him, but Antonelli. In his sunny Italian home he had led a peaceful, happy life, all his cares and ambition being centred in the little vineyard, the income from which was all sufficient to supply his family with every needed comfort. His first great sorrow came to him many years ago in the death of his wife, who left him one child, a daughter, named Angela, then nearly grown up.

In the course of time Angela married, and, as the old man's home would be desolate without his child, the young couple resided with him. Now everything seemed to point him to an old age of quiet and rest, even from his light labors and responsibilities, for Pedro could take charge of the vineyard. But Pedro was not one to be content with such a life of obscurity and inaction, and, while he patiently trimmed the vines, he dreamed of the fresh, vigorous new world across the waters, and longed to carry thither his now buried talents, and earn for himself a place among the illustrious of the world. All this Antonelli soon discovered, and, as he contrasted his son-in-law with those around them, he could not deny that he was fitted to fill a grander sphere than that in which he himself had so contentedly passed his life. Thus it came to pass that, when his daughter's first-born (little Luigi) was a few months old, he reluctantly consented to convert his property into gold, and emigrate with his entire family to America.

They had been at sea but a few days when they discovered among their fellow passengers a countryman of their own, a mere youth. He, too, was seeking the El Dorado of the West, but with more humble aspirations than those which moved our little party ; for all his hopes were centred in the fine-toned hand organ which was his constant companion.

While yet out of sight of land, the poor boy was taken sick. Pedro, who had become much interested in the young stranger, pitying his friendless condition, devoted himself untiringly to him, striving by every means in his power to alleviate his sufferings. On the third day the boy died, leaving to his benefactor his only earthly possession, his much-loved organ. But alas ! it soon became apparent that Pedro had sacrificed his life to his disinterested benevolence. He had caught the fever of which the youth had died, and the very day on which the first glimpse of the New World, for which he had so ardently longed, appeared above the horizon, his body was committed to the waves. His spirit had already reached that blest land where there are no disappointed aspirations, no blighted hopes, no tears, and no more death.

The bereaved family landed at New York without any definite aim or purpose before them. The old man, homesick and heartsick, fell in with one who spoke fair words to him in his much-loved native tongue, and in-duced him to intrust to his care the gold for which he had sold his little vineyard, the sole inheritance of his children. When too late he found that he had confided in a villain. His pretended friend suddenly disappeared, leaving him penniless. Misfortunes gathered thick and fast, till at last blindness was added to the many afflictions of the aged Italian. It was then that the humble legacy of the emi-grant boy became the only means of support to the little family, who were fast sinking to the lowest depths of poverty.

When poor old Antonelli had finished his story, and wiped away the tears which its recital had drawn from his sightless eyes, he raised the organ to his shoulders, gave Eva his hand, and they again commenced their wanderings.

As Eva, when the sunlight faded, made her way back to Mrs. Jenkins' fruit stand, and delivered her aged charge once more to her kind care, and then turned her steps homeward, her little limbs felt very weary from her long, tiresome walk, but her heart was light and joyful. And well it might be : Faith and Hope had long been her companions, and that day another of the celestial sisterhood had taken her by the hand, leading her many steps onward in the straight and narrow path which leadeth to life eternal : Faith, Hope, and *Charity*, these three ; but the greatest of these is *Charity*."

CHAPTER XIV.

IT was the day before Christmas. Little Eva had been to make her daily visit to her sister, and now she went tripping down Broadway with so much joyousness sparkling in her eyes and dimpling her lips, that a stranger would have supposed she expected Santa Claus to come tumbling down the chimney, with a whole sleigh-load of toys and candies for her especial benefit. But her happiness had a very different source. In the first place, Lilian was better—a great deal better. She had even been able to sit up a few minutes while the little girl was at the hospital. And then, were not her nimble feet bearing her on an errand of love and charity? The blind man, she knew, was awaiting his little guide, and her heart was filled with happiness that she could do some good in the world, in humble imitation of

8

Him, the Child of Bethlehem, who went about doing good.

She found the poor old Italian beside Mrs. Jenkins' fruit stand. He too looked more hopeful and happy than Eva had ever before seen him. The kind physician had kept his promise, and been to see little Luigi. The remedies he prescribed, and which he administered himself, were no homœopathic doses, I assure you. They consisted principally of a load of coal, comfortable beds and bedding, and a quantity of wholesome food. All these comforts the old man and his daughter shared with the sick child, and, to add to their thankfulness, he had brought home more money the day that Eva had led him through those pleasant streets than in any three days on which he had stood wearily turning the crank of his organ in noisy Broadway.

The old man and the child started off on their musical pilgrimage again, and Mrs. Jenkins forced each to take an apple from her stand to eat on the way.

Eva thought it would not be well to go over the same streets they passed through the day before, so she went a little farther up town, and turned into a splendid avenue, where she remembered walking with Lilian one afternoon in the summer when Mrs. Benton had given her a half holiday. They stopped before the first house they came to, and the blind man played. Pretty soon a window was opened, and a piece of money thrown out. It happened to fall in the snow, and while Eva looked for it her companion gave another tune by way of thanks. This chanced to be the " Portuguese Hymn," and as they walked on Eva caught up the strain, her sweet young voice floating out on the frosty air, with the words of the hymn, " The Lord is my Shepherd, no want shall I know," which she had learned at Sunday school to sing to that beautiful tune.

The Italian, with the quick ear for music peculiar to his nation, stopped short, and, motioning her to continue singing, listened with evident delight. When the song was concluded, he exclaimed rapturously, " Ah, the sweet voice! me not know little Eva can sing so like the angels; " then, a new and somewhat mercenary thought striking him, he continued eagerly, "If little Eva sing when me play, the people give more money. Will she ? "

" Why, Mr. Antonelli," replied the little girl, laughing, " that would be just like expecting people to pay me for singing. Who ever heard of such a thing ? "

"Everybody have heard of such a thing; do not you know of the opera and the concerts?"

"Oh, yes! but that seems different. I will sing, though, Mr. Antonelli, if you think it would help you any."

◦ "No, no, not at all to help me; if you sing, then you must take half the moneys," said the old man.

To this Eva would not consent; but, after much discussion, it was finally agreed that, if the organ grinder received anything more than he did the day before, the overplus should be equally divided between the two.

This one hymn was the only tune with which Eva and the organ were mutually acquainted, so it formed a part of the performance at every place they stopped. Sometimes the audience, gathered at the windows, would call upon the child to sing again, and then Antonelli would cease his grinding, while she gave one of the simple songs with which she was familiar. At two or three houses they were called into the hall, and, while the admiring household gathered around, song after song issued from Eva's ruby lips, filling the whole house with melody. Then they were sure not to be dismissed empty-handed. The old man's pocket contained more silver than it had held for many a day; and as for our little Eva, she grew quite excited. Wild, impossible-to-be-performed projects of making a fortune for herself and all her friends filled her brain. She thought of Jenny Lind and all the great singers she had ever heard of, and began to wonder if she was not to be one of them.

The day was almost done; jets of gas were already sending forth their brilliant light through the windows of stately mansions which they passed, though in the west there were still lingering traces of the beautiful sunset. On the calm beauty of the fleecy clouds Eva's eyes were fixed, as she silently led her equally silent companion. The worldly ambition which had so stirred her young heart was fading away, and a calm contentment took its place as she watched the first star of the evening break from behind a light cloud, and remembered that the same gracious God, who by the leading of a star brought the wise men to the knowledge of His Son, whom He had sent into the world with the gift of life immortal, still guided and directed all things, and knew how to give unto His children such good gifts as were needful for them.

Presently the child slackened her pace,

and, looking up to the old man, said, "We
will stop here and play and sing once more;
then we must go home, for it is growing
late."

The spot she had selected for this "posi-
tively the last entertainment" of the evening
was where the light from an illuminated parlor fell directly upon them. While the blind
man is playing a prelude, we will look in
upon the family group gathered within the
parlor. The room is dressed for Christmas;
graceful festoons of evergreens drape the
walls and droop from the ceiling. By the
bright coal fire is seated a gentleman, engaged in telling a story to two little boys.
They seem much interested in the story, but
yet their eyes will every now and then wander longingly toward the folding doors that
shut the next room from their view, from
which they can hear the sound of merry
voices and quick footsteps.

Near one of the windows is standing a
young girl, amusing herself by watching the
passers-by. There is a look of pleased ex-
pectancy on her face, and she too, like her
brothers, from time to time casts a glance of
impatient curiosity toward those tantalizing
doors.

The music of our old man's organ, as it

floated through the room, attracted but little . attention from the fireside group, until the young girl exclaimed, " Oh, do come, papa, and see what a beautiful child! Don't her golden curls, falling over her black dress, look exactly like a flood of sunshine lighting up a cloud; and isn't that a romantic looking old man with her!"

" That is because he is seen through a pair of romantic young eyes, Isabell," replied her father, laughing; " but the child certainly is pretty, and hark! what a sweet voice she has."

They stood listening in silence, while Eva sang, to the really fine music of the organ, her beautiful hymn " The Lord is my Shepherd, no want shall I know." " That little girl's face seems very familiar to me," said Mr. Grey thoughtfully, as the last note of the hymn died away; then, as struck by some sudden recollection, he hurried to the door and beckoned Eva to him. She came quickly up the steps, and he, placing his hand kindly on her head, asked, " Have I not seen you before, little one?"

Eva looked up at him a moment, then, as an expression of glad recognition lighted up her face, she exclaimed:

" Oh yes! sir; it was you who gave me dear little Faith."

"How do you know that it was I who gave it to you?" he asked, smiling.

"Because, sir, it came with the dishes, and no one else could have sent it," replied Eva; then, in a timid voice, she continued, "I have wanted, a great many times, to see you and thank you, but now I don't know how to thank you half enough."

"Never mind the thanks," said Mr. Grey, as he seated himself and drew her toward him, "I think on the whole you have paid off all obligation on that score. Let me see; I gave you an image of Faith, and you have just given me a song of Faith; so we are about even; don't you think so?"

Eva shook her head slowly, but before she could venture upon any more decided dissent from the gentleman's sagely expressed opinion, one of the boys who had followed his father into the hall and had been an eager listener to all that was said, broke in upon the conversation, by exclaiming, "Why, papa, is this the little girl you was telling us about seeing in the china store? Isn't it funny that she should happen to come just when we were talking about her?"

Old Antonelli was called in, and while he sat in the hall enjoying the cup of hot coffee and plate of nice sandwiches which Isabelle thoughtfully provided for him, Eva, in answer to Mr. Grey's questions, told of all that had befallen herself and her sister since the day he had talked with her about faith, while Lilian was making her first purchases in the great city.

"Have you no brother?" asked Freddie, the eldest of the boys, as Eva finished her story.

"No," she replied; "I did have one, when I was a baby, but he went to sea with my uncle in his ship, and they were both drowned."

"Is not your name Ross?" inquired Mr. Grey, suddenly.

"Yes, sir, Eva Ross."

"And your uncle's name, who was lost at the same time with your brother?"

"John Marvin, sir," replied Eva, while Freddie looked inquiringly at his father, wondering why he questioned the little girl with so much apparent interest.

"Aha! John Marvin," repeated Mr. Grey, catching up a newspaper and turning it over, as if looking for something; then, with his finger on the paragraph which he had sought, he asked, "Do you know what your uncle's ship was called?"

"Yes, sir; it was named Mary Ross, after mamma," returned Eva, beginning to wonder,

8*

as well as Freddie, why he seemed so much interested in the matter.

"Then listen to this!" exclaimed Mr. Grey; and he read from the newspaper, "The heirs of the late Captain John Marvin, of the ship 'Mary Ross,' who, with his vessel and all on board, was lost at sea in the year 1849, will hear something to their advantage, by applying to A. Jones, No. —— —— st."

Eva could not exactly understand what it all meant, but Mr. Grey explained to her, that the Captain Marvin referred to in the paragraph was evidently her own uncle; that she and her sister were his heirs, or those to whom his property would rightfully belong, after his death; and that it was probable the advertiser, A. Jones, had in his possession, or knew of, some property which had belonged to Captain Marvin, and to which they were consequently entitled.

" Oh, isn't that nice!" exclaimed Freddie; " she won't have to go out in the cold, to earn money, any more, will she, papa?"

" It is just like what we read about in books," added Isabelle, delighted at finding even so simple a specimen of romance in real life.

"I am so glad she happened to come here!" cried little Charlie, dancing about with joy, that some good fortune, though he could not comprehend what, had befallen the young stranger.

Eva alone said nothing; above all this friendly clamor there was sounding in her ears the words she had sung so many times that day, "The Lord is my Shepherd, no want shall I know."

"Wait, children, wait," said Mr. Grey, smiling; "you are too quick with your conclusions; we do not know yet what it is this Mr. Jones has to tell; suppose I go and see him now, so as to satisfy our curiosity as soon as possible."

"Oh yes! oh do, papa!" they all exclaimed, and Eva's blue eyes spoke as plainly as they could in favor of the proposal.

"Run, Charlie, and ask you mamma if I shall have time to go to ——— street and back again, before Santa Claus has finished the tree."

Charlie bounded away with his father's message, and soon returned, saying that his mamma thought there would be more than time enough.

"Then I will be off, and this little girl had better wait here to hear the news."

"Oh no, sir; I cannot stay any longer, I must take Mr. Antonelli home; and besides,

Mrs. Havens will think I am lost, if I am out so late; but mayn't I come to-morrow and hear about it?"

"That is right, child; always think of your duty to others before your own gratification. Certainly you shall come to-morrow and hear all that I can learn about the matter."

"But, papa," said Charlie, not at all satisfied with this decision; "I want her to see our Christmas tree!"

"Sure enough! well thought of, my boy. Let me see how we can arrange it;" then, taking the little girl's hand in his, as she stood before him, Mr. Grey continued, "You, Eva, can lead your blind friend back to his stand in Broadway, then go home to satisfy Mrs. Havens that you are safe, and when I have seen Mr. Jones, I will come for you and bring you here,. to see what kind of fruit grows on a Christmas tree."

"Oh, that will be nice! It takes papa to get folks out of a fix!" cried Charlie, clapping his hands, while little Eva's bright smile and softly spoken "Thank you, sir," sufficiently testified her joy.

"Had she not better tell her friends that she will stay here all night?" asked Isabelle; "you know, papa, it will be so late for her to go home."

"That will be a very good plan, daughter, if she is willing to stay. How is that, my little girl?" he asked, turning to Eva.

"I should like to stay," answered the child, simply, laying her little hand in Isabelle's. How short the walk seemed to Mrs. Jenkins' fruit stand, and how the good woman rolled up her eyes and declared she "Neber heard nothin' like it afore in all her life," when Eva hastily told of her adventure. The old blind man urged the little songstress to take her share of their day's earnings, which she refused to do, saying, "Who knows but that the gentleman who put it in the paper about Uncle John, has some money for Lillie and me, and then I won't need it."

"Ah, but if he not have any moneys for you? what then, carissima?"

"Then I will go and sing with you again and make some more," replied Eva, as she bounded away, laughing.

Arrived at home, she met Mrs. Havens in the hall, who exclaimed, in her most querulous tones, "What on earth has kept you out so late, child? I have been worried almost to death about you; I don't see any use in your going out at all now any way, for I am sure you can't have anything to sell."

As soon as Eva could find a chance to

speak, she laid her hand coaxingly on Mrs.
Havens' arm, saying, " I am very sorry you
were troubled about me. I will try not to be
so late again ; " then briefly told her how she
had passed the day, and of the crowning adventure of the evening.

"Well, I never ! " exclaimed the land-
lady, somewhat mollified ; " you are the
queerest child I ever did see. The idea of
your going about the streets singing, with an
old organ grinder ! I wonder what your sister would say ! But I hope the story about
your uncle's property will turn out well,
though I don't know," and she shook her head
doubtingly. " Well, child," she resumed, " if
you are going to that Christmas tree, or whatever it is, you had better run up stairs now,
and change your dress. I will send Jennie to
help you fix your hair. I don't believe those
useless curls have been real smooth and tidy
once since Lilian has been sick, though I dare
say you have worked hard enough to make
them so, poor child ! so you need not look so
distressed about it."

It did not take our little heroine long to
decide upon her toilette, as she had but one
dress besides that she had on—the one made
from Aunty Smith's old bombazine, which,
with careful treatment, still did duty very

respectably as her best. Jennie, " clothed in
a little brief authority," pulled dreadfully in
getting the tangles out of her curls, but the
child had been so shocked at Mrs. Havens' in-
sinuation that she did not look tidy, that she
bore the' torture like a stoic, and even promised Jennie that, if she should get any candy
from the tree, she would give her half, as a
reward for her services.

When at last the troublesome curls hung
in smooth, glistening clusters over her shoulders, she laid Dolly on the bed, " to make her
look comfortable," kissed little Faith, and
wishing Jennie a merry Christmas, soon stood,
hooded and cloaked, watching for Mr. Grey
through the side light of the front door. She
had not waited long when a sleigh drove up,
and in another moment she was sitting, wrapped in soft robes, beside her kind friend, who
was telling her the result of his visit to Mr.
Jones. It appeared that Captain Marvin,
just before he sailed on his last voyage, had
authorized Mr. Jones to collect some debts
that were owing him, during his absence.
The money was collected, but the owner did
not return, and when news came of his loss at
sea, Mr. Jones placed the money in bank and
advertised for the heirs. Receiving no response to the advertisement, he still continued

to have it inserted in the papers several times
each year, hoping that at last it might meet
the eye of some one interested. It so happened
that neither the orphans, nor any of their
friends in the remote little village of B——,
had chanced to see the notice, and but for
Eva's charitable effort to assist the old blind
man, they might never have known of the
good fortune that awaited them.

The property was not very large, but it
would be amply sufficient to support our
young friends in their simple, economical
habits, even allowing them something to give
away to those less fortunate.

When Mr. Grey had explained this to the
child as simply and briefly as possible, she
exclaimed, joyfully, " Then sister Lillie won't
have to sew, sew, sew all the time when she
gets well, and I can go to school again ; oh, I
am so glad ! "

" Here they come! here they come ! "
shouted Freddie and Charlie, darting from the
window, and rushing tumultuously to the
door, as the sleigh containing their father
and their little guest drove up. They seized
Eva, and drew her, in triumph, to the parlor,
exclaiming, " There, mamma, we told you
papa would bring her back, and here she is ! "
The child was somewhat abashed at finding

MR. GREY'S HOUSEHOLD.

herself so unceremoniously ushered into the midst of a numerous company (for all Freddie's and Charlie's uncles, aunts, and cousins had arrived, and formed quite a large party), but the lady whom the boys addressed as mamma, gently reproving them for their thoughtlessness, received her with a kiss and a few kind words of welcome, and then gave her in charge of Isabelle, with whom she at once felt at ease.

Isabelle led her up stairs to her own room, took off her cloak and hood, and showed her the nice little bed that had been prepared for her close to hers. When they returned to the parlor they found the whole company, from Mr. Grey down to little Charlie, preparing for a romping game of "Blind man's buff." Eva entered with all her heart into the sport; she laughed as merrily and bounded over the velvet carpet with as light and careless grace as any of the little children there, though *they* had never known a ruder playground, or encountered a greater difficulty than that of eluding the grasp of "Cousin Will," who, with bandaged eyes and outstretched arms, came so very near catching somebody, but never quite succeeded. Then came "Magic Music," "Hunt the slipper," and "Forfeits," and at last, just as the children were wondering what they should do next, the folding-doors were thrown open, and there stood the Christmas tree, with its tiny tapers, its glittering balls, and all the countless beautiful things which loving hands had hung upon its branches.

"Oh, isn't it beautiful!" exclaimed glad young voices, amid the clapping of little hands; but Eva neither spoke nor moved; she had never before seen anything like it, and it seemed to her so like a dream, that she scarce dared breathe, lest it should vanish away.

"What do you think of it, Eva?" asked Mrs. Grey, drawing her to her side.

"Oh, you were so good to let me come and see it!" was the child's only reply, as she pressed her lips, quivering with excitement, on Mrs. Grey's hand, somewhat to that lady's surprise. Just then Freddie came to lead her to a place in the procession, which was forming, to walk around the tree, that all might view it at every point—a very merry procession it was, I assure you. When the ceremony was over, Mr. Grey, mounted on a set of library steps, proceeded to strip the heavily laden branches of the Aladdin-like tree. To each article was attached the name of the person for whom it was intended, which Mr. Grey read aloud as he presented it. "Eva

Ross," he presently called out; and, the child stepping timidly forward, he placed in her hands a beautifully carved musical box. He touched the stops as he gave, it to her, and the clear, sweet notes of the "Portuguese Hymn" mingled with the sounds of innocent merriment that filled the room. Soon her name was called again, and this time it was an enormous cornucopia. She had just made her way back to Isabelle with her treasure, thinking how pleasant it would be to redeem her promise to Jennie Havens, by sharing with her the contents of this beautiful horn of plenty, when, to her surprise, she heard her sister's name. At first she thought she must be mistaken; but no—" Lilian Ross," repeated Mr. Grey, and Isabelle told her that, as her sister was not present, she must take charge of whatever Santa Claus had left for her. It was a graceful little basket, filled with large bunches of luscious grapes, white and purple, tastefully interspersed with sprigs of holly. This thoughtful care for her sick sister touched the sensitive child more deeply even than all the kindness to herself, and she could scarce keep back the tears of gratitude, as she whispered her thanks.

The happiest day, as well as the saddest, must have an end, and so at length, ·when

every one had enjoyed their full of fun and
frolic, the uncles and aunts and cousins de-
parted amid a shower of kisses and good-bys,
while everybody wished everybody else a
merry Christmas.

˙ How soundly Eva slept that night, in the
snug little bed prepared for her ; and how,
when she awoke bright and early in the
morning, she looked about in bewildered surprise, wondering where she was and how she
came there, till an amused laugh from Isabelle made it all clear again.

"Oh," she exclaimed, joining in the
laugh ; "I thought that all about the tree
was a dream, and couldn't quite make out
whether I was awake yet or not."

When the family were gathered together
for morning prayers, Mr. Grey talked very
seriously to the children about the day whose
coming had made them all so glad. He told
them that Christmas day should not be alto-
gether devoted to mirth and festivity. That
we should think of Him whose birth it com-
memorates, and try to grow like Him ; that
as He gave to us the inestimable gifts of His
atoning blood, His life and His example, so
we too should give gifts, not only pretty presents to friends and relatives—though this is
right, as showing love and good-will one to

another—but comforts and necessities to the poor and needy. That as He was meek and lowly, so should we put away all pride, vanity, and self-righteousness; that as He forgave His enemies, and prayed for them who despitefully used Him, we likewise should forgive all those who have injured us, and on this day, when angels sung of peace and good-will, commence life anew in love and charity with all; then we should be very sure of a happy, if not a merry Christmas.

At the breakfast table a new surprise awaited our little heroine. Beneath each plate was a small parcel enclosing some appropriate gift. Freddie, Charlie, and Eva each had, alike, a pretty pearl portemonnaie, containing two gold dollars.

The boys prattled the whole meal time as to how they should spend their money. Eva said nothing, after a few embarrassed words of thanks (embarrassed because she did not exactly know to whom they should be spoken); but she had mentally disposed of her two dollars long before Masters Freddie and Charlie, with all their talking, had decided what to do with theirs. Dr. H—— had told her that she might come earlier and stay longer with Lilian to-day, as it was Christmas; and very soon after breakfast she

was ready to go, with a covered basket on
her arm, in which Lilian's basket of grapes
and her own music box and cornucopia were,
with Isabelle's assistance, carefully packed
for safe carrying. When she went to seek
Mr. and Mrs. Grey to say good-by, she found
them standing before the dining-room fire,
evidently engaged in some important consult-
ation. Mrs. Grey, as soon as she saw the
child, held out her hand to her, saying,
" What! going so soon, little Eva ? "

" Yes, ma'am," she replied, approaching ;
" but I will come back to bring the basket
by-and-by."

Mrs. Grey smiled, and asked, " Won't you
come and stay with us, Eva—you and your
sister—until she gets quite well again ? "

" And will you bring sister Lillie here ? "
cried the little girl, scarce believing that she
had heard aright.

" Certainly, my dear, we will bring her
here this very day if the physician says it
will do no harm to move her."

Eva's sparkling eyes told the thanks she
could not speak ; and her kind friends, promising to meet her at the hospital early in the
afternoon, let her go to tell her sister all the
happiness that filled her heart.

" You will come back again ; mamma

says so," said Freddie and Charlie, as they parted, after escorting her down the steps.

"Yes, and Lillie is coming too. Won't we have nice times?" replied the child, artlessly, as she hurried away. She walked rapidly until she came to a florist's greenhouse; here she stopped, and, with part of one of her gold dollars, purchased a beautiful bouquet, which she placed carefully in the basket, and, again starting off with a quick step, she was not long in reaching the hospital.

Lilian was sitting up when she arrived, and great was her surprise when the delighted child placed in her lap the basket of grapes, and, holding up the flowers, said softly, as she kissed her, "See, sister, I have brought you a merry Christmas!"

"Why, darling," she said, drawing her close to her side, "where did you get these beautiful things?"

"Mr. Grey, the gentleman who gave me little Faith, you know, sent the grapes, and I bought the flowers myself. Ar'n't they sweet!"

Lilian looked more puzzled than ever at this explanation. Then Eva related all her adventures of the last few days (her wanderings with old Antonelli she had, until now, kept secret from her sister, lest she should be alarmed for her safety). The sick girl listened in amazement, till Eva told how, the day before, she went from house to house singing, when, folding her arms more tightly around her, she exclaimed, almost reproachfully, " And all the time I thought you were safe at home, under Mrs. Havens' care ! "

" Sister," said the little girl, in a low tone, laying her head on Lilian's shoulder, " God took care of me. Listen how He led me to good, kind friends ; " and then she told of her stopping before Mr. Grey's house, and all that had resulted from it.

Lilian kissed her in silence, while tears of thankfulness rolled down her pale cheeks. When Dr. H—— came, he readily gave his consent that his young patient should be removed to Mr. Grey's, saying. there would be no danger if she was properly wrapped up and moved with care. So, when Mr. and Mrs. Grey arrived in a close carriage, well provided with pillows and blankets, she was carried out, placed in it, and driven slowly away.

Mr. Grey and Eva stood watching until the carriage and its precious burden was lost sight of in the throng. Then he asked if she would like to go anywhere else before returning home with him. Now Eva wished very much to spend the remainder of her money in Christmas presents for Mrs. Jenkins and the poor Italian family, and so she told Mr. Grey. He laughed at the thought of her doing so much with so small a sum. But Eva had decided what to buy and counted the cost, and easily convinced him that she did not expect to perform impossibilities. First she wanted a picture book for Luigi, who was now getting well enough to need some amusement; then a pound of tea for his mother, a pair of warm stockings for the blind man, and for Mrs. Jenkins a pretty china sugar bowl. She had decided upon this last from observing that the good woman's tea set was minus such an article, its place being supplied by a cracked tumbler.

When the purchases were made, Mr. Grey went with the little girl to distribute her gifts. They first visited poor old Antonelli's cheerless abode. It was less desolate than on Eva's former visit, owing to the good doctor's bounty, but the child and her kind friend left it brighter still; for, in addition to her very acceptable gifts, Mr. Grey placed in the old man's hand a well-filled purse, and promised to procure him some better means of earning a living than by his organ grinding. They

9

found Mrs. Jenkins, Cato, and Sally just finishing their Christmas dinner. The savory fumes of the roast goose and plum pudding testified to its having been a good one. The simple souls were overjoyed to see Eva, though somewhat abashed at the presence of Mr. Grey. He, however, soon set them at ease by his pleasant, friendly manner, and, before he had been in the room many minutes, old Cato was telling him all about his rheumatism as freely as if he had known him for years. Eva's sugar bowl was received with loud demonstrations of delight and admiration. Cato declared that the sugar " dat comed out ob it would be de very sweetest sugar in de whole worl'," and his wife said she should " keep it jes' as long as she lived, ter 'member de darlin' little rosebud what gave it to her."

When Eva had bid her humble friends good-by, and made them very happy by promising to come and take tea with them soon, Mr. Grey said he thought that they had best go and see Mrs. Havens, as she might wonder what had become of her little lodger. That was just what Eva had been thinking of, and besides, she wanted to give Jennie the candy ; so she gladly agreed to the proposal.

"Would you not like to see 'little Faith' again?" she asked, looking up in his face. "Mayn't I take it to your house, and my doll too?" He gave a laughing assent as he rang Mrs. Havens's doorbell.

Mrs. Havens received Mr. Grey in her solemn front parlor, and listened with real pleasure as he told of the good fortune that had befallen the orphans, and of his wife's intention to take charge of them until Lilian's health should be restored. In the mean time Jennie, who had accompanied Eva up stairs to get her treasures, was listening with wonder to her account of the last night's festivities, and devouring the contents of the cornucopia.

Dolly was soon dressed in her street costume, the little statuette carefully placed in a pasteboard box, and Eva stood by Mr. Grey's side, ready to accompany him to his pleasant home, where her sister was already awaiting her. Mrs. Havens gave her a kiss, telling her she must come to-morrow and help pack her own and Lilian's clothes, which were to be sent to them at Mr. Grey's. She promised to be there early in the morning, and in a moment more was walking quickly through the street, with her hand resting confidingly in that of her kind protector.

"Well, I declare!" sighed Mrs. Havens, as she stood looking after them; "some people seem born to good luck. Who would have thought, when I was worrying about those children, along with all my own troubles, that they would be so well provided for all at once? And it all comes of that little imp's outlandish doings, too!" she added, with something very like a smile, as she closed the door, and sat down to count the bills which Mr. Grey had insisted upon her taking, in payment of a quarter's rent for the room which the orphans had occupied, because, as he said, he was robbing her of her lodgers without giving notice.

Isabelle and the boys gladly welcomed Eva back again. They had been watching for her ever since their mother returned with Lilian, and wondering what kept her and their father so long.

Freddie had his books and Charlie his toys all ready for her entertainment, and were for carrying her off to their playroom as soon as she made her appearance; but she drew back, saying, "I will like to go with you pretty soon, but can't till I see Lillie first."

"Oh, sure enough; I forgot," exclaimed Freddie.

"You see, brother mine, there is such a thing as being too hospitable," said Isabelle, pleasantly, as she took Eva's hand and led her to her sister's room. A very pleasant room it was. The soft carpet gave back no sound from the footfall, heavy crimson curtains shaded the windows, and a bright, cheerful fire glowed in the grate. Lilian, pale and exhausted, but otherwise none the worse for her ride, reclined on the downy couch. Mrs. Grey, seated in an easy chair by her side, was bathing her brow, while a servant was noiselessly engaged in arranging, on the opposite side of the room, the same little bed that Eva had occupied the night before.

Eva was not allowed to stay long, as Mrs. Grey said it was best that Lilian should try to sleep after her fatigue; so she went to join the boys in the playroom, well satisfied that her sister could want for nothing while under such kind guardianship.

What a fine time the children had together, and how astonished the boys were when at last told that it was dinner time!

"Why, this is the shortest day I ever knew!" said Freddie, as they went down stairs.

"Yes," replied Charlie; "only the time we

were watching for papa and Eva didn't seem very short."

"That must have been because you had nothing to do but watch," said Eva; "for that very same time seemed short to me, because I was going around to so many places, and seeing so many different people."

"And yet," said Freddie, thoughtfully, "papa once told me that it is not the number of days or years that a person lives that makes their life long or short, but the number of deeds they perform. He said that the busiest life was the longest; so I should think that idle time would be the shortest."

Eva looked puzzled. She was sure that Freddie's reasoning was not correct, but did not know how to explain the matter. "It does seem odd," she said, shaking her head doubtfully.

"I'll ask papa; he can tell us how it is," cried Freddie, leading the way to the dining room, where they soon had their philosophical enigma unravelled over the Christmas turkey.

"Has not this been a real merry Christmas?" said Charlie to his brother, as they parted from their little guest for the night.

"Yes, indeed it has," replied Freddie, heartily. Eva thought so too; and, when she knelt to offer up her simple prayers and thanksgivings, she did not forget to thank the Giver of *all* good gifts for the little pleasures as well as the great benefits which had made it for her a merry Christmas.

CHAPTER XV.

Do my young readers wish to look in upon little Eva once more, just to say good-by before parting? If so, they must come with me again to the pretty village of B——. It is near the close of a beautiful day in spring. Eva is seated on the steps of the porch in front of the little white cottage—her well-remembered, much-loved home. By her side is old Ponto, his great head resting on her knee, to the no small peril of the flowers she holds in her lap, and from which she is arranging bouquets for the vases which stand on the step above her. The setting sun lights up the scene with a mellow glow. The birds are twittering low and lovingly to one another, as they take advantage of the few last streaks of sunlight to see that all is right with the little ones in their snug nest away up in the branches of the old elm tree, whose graceful boughs have so long sheltered the cottage alike from summer suns and winter blasts. The child looks up from her flowers every few moments to gaze eagerly down the road, as if expecting some one.

Within doors all looks bright and cheerful. The furniture of the parlor is the same as in the old time, with the exception of some few articles of more modern make and graceful form, which add at once to the tastefulness and comfort of the little room. Lilian, who has just spread a snowy cloth on the small, round tea-table, takes from the closet a dainty set of French china. "A present from Mrs. Grey," she says, in answer to an exclamation of admiration from Miss Jackson, who has for the last few moments been peering out the window in the same direction as that to which Eva's eyes so constantly turn, and who draws in her head just as the last plate is laid on the table. By the way, the table is set for four, though Miss Jackson, Lilian, and Eva are at present the only persons about the house.

"Well, seems to me those city folks ar'n't any ways mean in giving presents," exclaimed the cheery little woman, as she examined the delicate tracery of one of the cups. "I don't know how many beautiful things

9*

you have got about here that eithei Mr. or
Mrs. or Miss Grey gave to you. Let me see ;
there is the picture over the mantelpiece, and
your workbox, and Eva's writing desk, and
all those beautiful books, and "— But Miss
Jackson's inventory was cut short by a joyful shout from Eva, who, springing up re-
gardless of Ponto's comfort or the safety of
her flowers, bounded to the gate, crying out,
" She is coming ! she is coming ! "

Lilian and Miss Jackson hurried to the
door. Yes ! there it came at last—the stage
that they had been watching for so long—
sweeping up the road. It stopped before the
gate, and Miss Becky, dear Miss Becky herself sprang out, and, catching little Eva in
her arms, almost smothered her with kisses.

" Oh, I am so glad we are back in our
darling old home again," said Eva, when, the
first excitement of the meeting over, they
were all collected in Miss Becky's room ;
" and you are going to stay with us always,
ar'n't you ? " she added, as she wound her
plump arms around her friend's neck.

" Yes, just as long as you want me, precious one," replied Miss Becky, kissing her
for the twentieth time.

" Do you know, Miss Becky, I began to
fear you would disappoint us after all ? " said

Lilian. "We expected to find you when we arrived from New York; and Mr. and Mrs. Grey, who came with us, stayed two days later than they intended, hoping to see you; but yesterday they were obliged to go home; and, I assure you, they were very sorry not to see the dear, good friend, whom they had heard Eva and me talk só much about."

"Well, it won't be long before they see her," exclaimed Eva; "for oh, Miss Becky! they are coming to make us a visit this summer, and they will bring Isabelle and the boys too; won't it be delightful?"

. Miss Becky was in the midst of explaining the cause of her delay, when Miss Jackson made her appearance, and announced that tea was ready. Lilian had quite forgotten her housekeeping in the happiness of seeing her old friend, and the bustling little dressmaker had, unperceived by the others, slipped out of the room, and hurried to the kitchen, just in time to save the biscuits from being burnt and the tea from boiling over.

Eva laughed merrily at the idea of the company being obliged to get supper. But a very good supper it was, and fortunately the "company" was not ceremonious enough to let it spoil. The biscuit were as white as snow, the butter looked for all the world like a lump of gold; then the sponge cake, made by Lilian's own hands, was not to be surpassed by any French cook in existence, and the honey—well, we must give the bees credit for that; and the bees who made that particular honey must have been proficients in their art.

While the little group around the table were discussing these good things, they talked of the various changes (they were not many) which had taken place in the village since they last met together. There was a new store around the corner; a terrible conflagration had destroyed the blacksmith's shop and Captain Giles's barn; there had been several deaths and a few weddings, and that was about all that had varied the quiet life of B——.

"Isn't there a new keeper at the toll-gate?" asked Miss Becky, when all these important events had been commented upon; "when the stage passed through to-day, I looked out, expecting to say 'How d'ye do' to Sam Green, but there was an old blind man taking the toll instead of Sam."

"Oh yes!" cried Eva; "that is my old organ grinder."

"What, the one you wrote me about,

Lilian ?" inquired Miss Becky ; "how came he here ?"

"Why, you see, Miss Becky, the poor old soul could not make much at organ grinding, especially when he did not have Birdie to sing for him," said Lilian, casting a fond yet laughing glance at Eva ; " and as he was unwilling to live on charity, Mr. Grey promised to find him some other employment. It was not very easy to procure work for a blind man, when so many able-bodied men were seeking it in vain, but Mr. Grey did not forget his promise, and when he came down here, several weeks ago, to see about getting this dear old house for us, he heard that the toll keeper was going to California to mend his fortunes, and so secured his place for old Antonelli."

" And it is just the best place in the world for him," added Eva ; " Luigi is growing real fat and strong, and his mother is a great deal better. They can help him collect the toll. And sometimes, on pleasant evenings, he takes his organ out on the green, and all the children gather about him, to hear the music, and there isn't any ugly noise to spoil it all, as there was in Broadway."

"What has become of your friend Mrs. Jenkins, whom Lilian mentioned in the same letter in which she told me about the Ital-

ians ? " asked Miss Becky, when they had left
the table, and Eva was seated on her lap, by
the window.

"She is in her old home yet; but her son
Tom is Mr. Grey's coachman, and he has such
good wages that he can help take care of his
father and mother, so Mrs. Jenkins don't have
to go out with her fruit, only in pleasant
weather. She says she would not like to give
it up entirely, for she should miss the bustle
and noise, and seeing the people pass. Oh,
she is a real nice woman, and when I go to
New York—Mrs. Grey says we must come
and visit them sometimes—I am going to take
her and Cato all kinds of nice good ' country
things ' to eat."

Long after Eva had said her prayers, and
Miss Becky's gentle hands had tucked the
bedclothes snugly around her that night, excitement kept her awake.

Her brain was teeming with plans of im-
provement and amusement. She was to commence going to school next week. How hard
she would study, and how careful she would be
not to transgress any of the rules! But after
school hours, what fine times she would have
with her old playmates! They would have
such pleasant picnics down by the brook;
and when the little girls came to visit her,

how nice it would be to show them the beautiful books and toys that she had brought from the city.

But while her thoughts were busy with these innocent visions, a silvery moonbeam suddenly shot through the vine-covered casement, and, falling upon the little statue of Faith, which stood on a stand near the window, brought out distinctly from the surrounding obscurity the beautiful figure, with its upturned face; and as the child gazed upon it, she resolved never to forget the lesson it had taught her, but, however rough her path through life might again become, to take up the cross, and patiently tread the flinty way, knowing that though it might not lead, as had the trials through which she had lately passed, to a peaceful, happy, earthly home, it would yet, if she faithfully watched for her Heavenly Father's beckoning hand through the darkness, and listened to his guiding voice amid the roar of the tempest, surely terminate in the green pastures beside the still waters of that blest home from whence there is no wandering.

THE END.

Juvenile Works.

A PLACE FOR EVERYTHING, and EVERYTHING IN ITS PLACE. By Cousin Alice. 16mo, illustrated, cloth, 75 c.

AMERICAN HISTORICAL TALES. 16mo, 75 cents.

APPLETON'S BOYS' AND GIRLS' AMERICAN ANNUAL for 1860. 1 vol. 12mo, illustrated. Cloth, gilt, $1 50.

AUNT KITTY'S TALES. By Maria J. McIntosh. 12mo, 75 cents.

AUNT FANNY'S STORY BOOK FOR LITTLE BOYS AND GIRLS. 18mo, illustrated, boards, 31 cents. Cloth, 38 cents.

BARON MUNCHAUSEN'S SURPRISING TRAVELS AND ADVENTURES. A new and beautiful edition. Illustrated with characteristic designs, by Crowquill. (Several colored.) 1 vol. 12mo. Extra cloth, gilt edges, $2 50.

BERTRAM NOEL. A Story for Youth. By E. J. May, author of "Louis' School Days," &c. 16mo, 75 cents.

BLIND ALICE. A Tale for Good Children. By Maria J. McIntosh. 1 vol. square 16mo, 38 cents.

BOYS (The) AT HOME. By the author of "Edgar Clifton." 16mo, illustrated, 75 cents.

BOY'S BOOK OF MODERN TRAVEL AND ADVENTURE. By Meredith Johnes. 1 neat vol. 16mo, illustrated, cloth, 75c.

BOYS' AND GIRLS' AMERICAN ANNUAL. Edited by T. Martin. With finely colored illustrations. 1 vol. 12mo, in extra cloth, gilt edges, $1 50.

BOY'S (The) BIRTH-DAY BOOK: a Collection of Tales, Essays, and Narratives of Adventures. By Mrs. S. C. Hall, William Howitt, Augustus Mayhew, Thomas Miller, G. A. Sala, &c., &c. 1 vol. crown 8vo, illustrated with 100 engravings. Cloth, gilt edges, $2.

BOY'S BOOK OF INDUSTRIAL INFORMATION. By Elisha Noyce, author of Outlines of Creation. Illustrated with 370 engravings. 12mo, extra cloth, $1 25.

BOY'S (The) OWN TOY MAKER. Square 16mo. 50 cents.

BIBLE STORIES: or, Tales from Scripture. 1 vol. square 12mo.

BOY'S OWN BOOK: a Complete Encyclopædia of all the Diversions, Athletic, Scientific, and Recreative, of Boyhood and Youth. New and enlarged edition, with numerous additional illustrations. 1 thick vol., extra cloth, $2.

Juvenile Works.

CHILDREN'S HOLIDAYS. A Story Book for the whole Year. 18mo, illustrated. Cloth, 50 cents.

CHILD'S FIRST HISTORY OF AMERICA. By the author of " Little Dora." Square 18mo, engravings. Half cloth, 25 cents.

CHILDREN'S (The) PICTURE GALLERY. Engravings from one hundred paintings by eminent English artists. 1 vol. 4to, $1 50.

DOUGLASS FARM. A Juvenile Story of Life in Virginia. By MARY E. BRADLEY. 16mo, illustrated. Cloth, 75 cents.

EDGAR CLIFTON; or, RIGHT and WRONG. 16mo. illus. 75 cents.

ELLEN LESLIE; or, the REWARD of SELF-CONTROL. By MARIA J. McINTOSH. 1 vol. square 16mo, 38 cents.

EMILY HERBERT; or, THE HAPPY HOME. By MARIA J. McINTOSH. 1 vol. square 12mo, 88 cents.

ENTOMOLOGY in SPORT and ENTOMOLOGY in EARNEST. By Two Lovers of the Science. 1 vol. 12mo. $1 25.

FAGGOTS for THE FIRESIDE; or, FACTS and FANCY. By Peter Parley. 1 vol. 12mo, beautifully illustrated, $1 12.

FLORENCE ARNOTT; or, IS SHE GENEROUS? By MARIA J. McINTOSH. 1 vol. square 16mo, 88 cents.

FUNNY STORY BOOK ; A LAUGHTER PROVOKING BOOK FOR YOUNG FOLKS. 16mo, illustrated, cloth, 75c. Extra cloth, gilt edges, $1.

GEORGE READY; or, HOW TO LIVE FOR OTHERS. By ROBERT O'LINCOLN. 16mo, illustrated. Cloth, 75 cents.

GOOD IN EVERY THING. By Mrs. BARWELL. Square 16mo, illustrated, 50 cents.

GRACE AND CLARA; or, BE JUST, as WELL AS GENEROUS. 1 vol. square 16mo, 88 cents.

GRANDMAMMA EASY'S TOY BOOKS. 8vo. colored. Per dozen, $1 50.

HEWET'S ILLUMINATED HOUSEHOLD STORIES FOR LITTLE FOLKS. Beautifully illustrated.

  No. 1. CINDERELLA,
  " 2. JACK THE GIANT KILLER.
  " 8. PUSS IN BOOTS.
  " 4. LITTLE RED RIDING HOOD.
  " 5. JACK AND THE BEAN STALK.
  " 6. TOM THUMB.
  " 7. BEAUTY AND THE BEAST. In fancy paper covers, each 25 cents. In fancy boards, each 50 cents.

Juvenile Books.

HISTORY OF PETER THE GREAT, CZAR OF RUSSIA. By SARAH H. BRADFORD. 16mo, illustrated, cloth, 75 cents.

HOUSEHOLD STORIES. Collected by the Brothers GRIMM Newly translated, embellished with 240 illustrations by Wehnert. 1 vol., cloth, $2 00. Gilt edges, $2 50.

HOWITT'S (MARY), SERIES of POPULAR JUVENILE WORKS. 14 vols. uniform, in a case, in extra cloth, neat style.

HOWITT'S (MARY), PICTURE AND VERSE BOOK, commonly called Otto Speckter's Fable Book. Illustrated with 100 plates. Cheap edition, 50 cents. Cloth, 63 cents. Gilt leaves, 75 cents.

JESSIE GRAHAM; or, FRIENDS DEAR, BUT TRUTH DEARER. By MARIA J. McINTOSH. 1 vol., square 16mo, 88 cents.

LITTLE DORA; or, THE FOUR SEASONS. By a Lady of Charleston. Beautifully illustrated, 25 cents. Cloth, 88 cents.

LITTLE FRANK, and other TALES. Square 16mo. Cloth, 25 cents.

LOSS AND GAIN; or, MARGARET'S HOME. By COUSIN ALICE.

LOUIS' SCHOOL DAYS. By E. J. MAY. Illustrated 16mo. 75 cents.

LOUISE; or, THE BEAUTY OF INTEGRITY, and other TALES. 16mo, boards, 25 cents. Cloth, 88 cents.

McINTOSH'S NEW JUVENILE LIBRARY. 7 beautiful vols. With illustrations. In a case, $2 50.

———————— META GRAY; or, What Makes HOME HAPPY? 16mo, cloth.

MARY LEE. A Story for the Young. By KATE LIVERMORE. 1 neat vol. 16mo, illustrated. Extra Cloth, 63 cents.

MARTHA'S HOOKS and EYES. 1 vol. 18mo, 37 cents.

MARRYATT'S SETTLERS IN CANADA. 2 vols. in one, colored, 62 cents.

———————— SCENES IN AFRICA. 2 vols. in one, colored 62 cents.

————————MASTERMAN READY. 8 vols in one, colored. 62 cents.

Juvenile Books.

MIDSUMMER FAYS: or, THE HOLIDAYS at WOODLEIGH. By SUSAN PINDAR. 1 vol. 16mo, 63 cents.

MORTIMER'S COLLEGE LIFE. With neat illustrations, 16mo, cloth, 75 cents. Extra cloth, gilt edges, $1.

MYSTERIOUS STORY BOOK; or, the GOOD STEPMOTHER. Illustrated, 16mo, cloth, 75 cents. Gilt edges, $1.

NEAL (ALICE B.) CONTENTMENT Better than WEALTH. 16mo, illustrated, 63 cents. Gilt edges, 90 cents.

———— PATIENT WAITING NO LOSS. 16mo, illustrated, 63 cents. Gilt edges, 90 cents.

———— NO SUCH WORD AS FAIL. 16mo, illustrated, 63 cents. Gilt edges, 90 cents.

———— "ALL'S NOT GOLD that GLITTERS," or, the YOUNG CALIFORNIAN. 1 vol. 16mo, neatly illustrated, 75 cents. Gilt edges, $1.

———— NOTHING VENTURE, NOTHING HAVE. 1 vol. 16mo, beautifully illustrated, 63 cents. Gilt edges, 90 cents.

———— OUT OF DEBT, OUT OF DANGER. 16mo, illustrated, cloth, 75 cents. Gilt edges, $1.

———— A PLACE for EVERYTHING. 16mo, cloth, 75 cents

———— THE COOPERS , or, GETTING UNDER WAY. 12mo, cloth, 75 cents.

NIGHT CAPS. By the author of "Aunt Fanny's Christmas Stories." 1 vol. 18mo, cloth, 50 cents.

NIGHT CAPS (The New). Told to Charley. By the author of "Aunt Fanny's Christmas Stories."

OUTLINES OF CREATION. By ELISHA NOYCE, author of "The Boy's Book of Industrial Information." 12mo, profusely illustrated, extra cloth, $1 50.

PARLEY'S PRESENT for ALL SEASONS. By S. G. GOODRICH, (Peter Parley.) Illustrated with 16 fine engravings. 12mo, elegantly bound in a new style, $1. Gilt edges, $1 25.

PELL'S GUIDE for THE YOUNG to Success and Happiness. 12mo, cloth, 38 cents. Extra cloth, gilt edges, 50 cents.

PHILIP RANDOLPH. A Tale of Virginia. By MARY GER-TRUDE. 18mo, 38 cents.

PICTURE PLEASURE BOOK (The). Illustrated by upwards of five hundred engravings from drawings by eminent artists. 4to. size, beautifully printed, on fine paper, and bound in fancy covers. First and Second Series, each $1 25.